GU00984105

# THE INCREDIBLE DIARY of...

## Kent

Edited By Machaela Gavaghan

First published in Great Britain in 2019 by:

Young Writers
Remus House
Coltsfoot Drive
Peterborough
PE2 9BF
Telephone: 01733 890066
Website: www.youngwriters.co.uk

All Rights Reserved
Book Design by Ashley Janson
© Copyright Contributors 2019
Softback ISBN 978-1-78988-677-1
Hardback ISBN 978-1-78988-978-9
Printed and bound in the UK by BookPrintingUK
Website: www.bookprintinguk.com
YB0411L

# ★ Foreword

Dear Reader,

You will never guess what I did today! Shall I tell you? Some primary school pupils wrote some diary entries and I got to read them, and they were EXCELLENT!

They wrote them in school and sent them to us here at Young Writers. We'd given their teachers some bright and funky worksheets to fill in, and some fun and fabulous (and free) resources to help spark ideas and get inspiration flowing.

And it clearly worked because WOW!! I can't believe the adventures I've been reading about. Real people, make-believe people, dogs and unicorns, even objects like pencils all feature and these diaries all have one thing in common – they are JAM-PACKED with imagination!

We live and breathe creativity here at Young Writers – it gives us life! We want to pass our love of the written word onto the next generation and what better way to do that than to celebrate their writing by publishing it in a book!

It sets their work free from homework books and notepads and puts it where it deserves to be – OUT IN THE WORLD! Each awesome author in this book should be **super proud** of themselves, and now they've got proof of their imagination, their ideas and their creativity in black and white, to look back on in years to come!

Now that I've read all these diaries, I've somehow got to pick some winners! Oh my gosh it's going to be difficult to choose, but I'm going to have SO MUCH FUN doing it!

Bye!

**Machaela**

# Contents

## Smarden Primary School, Smarden

| | |
|---|---|
| Sienna Jo Burns (10) | 84 |
| Tilda Goodwin (10) | 86 |
| Linden Hodgkins (10) | 87 |
| Scarlett Ida Adams (9) | 88 |
| Immy Barber (10) | 89 |
| Claire Flanagan (9) | 90 |
| Ebony Mansfield-Adams (10) | 91 |
| Isla Hardwick (10) | 92 |
| Millie Jane Jennings (10) | 93 |
| Ruby Perry (10) | 94 |

## St George's CE Primary School, Wrotham

| | |
|---|---|
| Amelie Rose Meynen (9) | 95 |
| Joshua Lemuel Miranda (9) | 96 |
| Alice Nuttall (9) | 98 |
| Eleanor Finley (8) | 100 |
| Morgan Gillham (9) | 102 |
| William Lambert (9) | 104 |
| Archie Wilgan (9) | 106 |
| Dalyn Robertson (9) | 108 |
| Hillary Konteng (8) | 109 |
| Nicholas Harry Patrick Waller (8) | 110 |
| Patience Climpson (8) | 111 |
| Gracie Critcher (8) | 112 |
| Matthew Hodges (9) | 113 |
| Teddy Dennis Henry Lingham (9) | 114 |
| Holly Hayler (9) | 115 |
| Curtis Heather (8) | 116 |

## West Minster Primary School, Sheerness

| | |
|---|---|
| Ronnie Richard Leslie (8) | 117 |
| Tia Tooley (8) | 118 |
| Lexie Johnson (8) | 120 |
| Amelia Rose Munday (8) | 122 |
| Tiana Johnson (8) | 124 |
| Arthur Michael Bancroft (8) | 126 |
| Alfie Preston (8) | 128 |

| | |
|---|---|
| Maicie Hill (10) | 130 |
| Anooshkan Anura Julian (10) | 131 |
| Joshua Smith (10) | 132 |
| Evie Joan Reid (11) | 134 |
| Tyler Amos (8) | 136 |
| Hayden Zwolinski (8) | 138 |
| Taylor Sheppard (10) | 139 |
| Jersi Noel (9) | 140 |
| Luke Stevens (10) | 142 |
| Lilli-Rai Guyver (8) | 143 |
| Tia Michelle Kelly Maria Morgan (10) | 144 |
| Shianne Berrisford (10) | 146 |
| Poppy-May Duchense (7) | 147 |
| Maddie Kulinski (9) | 148 |
| Tristan Pay (9) | 149 |
| Teddie William Pagett (9) | 150 |
| Maisey Jo Cooke (10) | 151 |
| Caitlin Harris (10) | 152 |
| Sophie Warwick (10) | 153 |
| Rosie McNeill (9) | 154 |
| Neelie Mcgow (8) | 155 |
| Kaydon Mitchell (7) | 156 |
| Dexter Wallis (8) | 157 |
| Isaac (8) | 158 |
| Sophie Emans (9) | 159 |
| Malachi Sands-Roache (7) | 160 |
| Millie Starling (8) | 161 |
| Joe Anthony Welch (8) | 162 |

# The Diaries

# The Incredible Diary Of... Greg Hessly

Dear Diary,

Early in the morning, I woke up and started getting ready for school. Then when I got my T-shirt, something flat came out of it. It was a ticket for the water park! I asked Mum if I could go instead of going to school, she said no. My brother, Rodrick, wanted to go with me so I came up with a plan. I told Rodrick my plan and he said he liked it, but he wanted to make it a bit more sneaky so he decided that we could drive in his band van to the water park.

I butted in and said, "But what if Mum finds out?" Rodrick said we could go to the local garage to make his van camouflage.

After all that was over, me and Rodrick were able to go to the water park.

When we got there, we were so, so, so excited but the problem was when the man asked us for the ticket because I left it at home. So then I drove the van all the way back home and when I got home, I realised Rodrick had the ticket! So he had loads of fun at the water park. Then I remembered I had the school play so I ran to school. Then we did the Kent test, I got 59/59!

**Fraser Dunn (7)**

Dymchurch Primary School, Romney Marsh
1

# The Incredible Diary Of... Simon Cowell

Dear Diary,

Today was very tough. Although most times were good, some were bad. This morning was perfect. I had my usual cooked breakfast, got dressed in my favourite jeans and a plain black top and checked my car to see if I had enough petrol to get to BGT. We were laughing about how long it was taking David. We couldn't stop giggling when he told us he couldn't find his underwear anywhere!

When all the spectators had arrived, it was time to judge. We did our entrances (like always, I was the best) and we took our seats as the crowd's applause faded.

We had seen four amazing auditions and one rubbish one. In the good auditions, we'd seen two singing, one comedy and one ventriloquist. In the bad auditions, we'd seen one rubbish magic show. Unexpectedly, for the sixth act, Taylor Swift walked on stage. I was so happy that we finally had a great singer, but when I saw she was wearing a crocodile outfit, I was curious. When she started doing comedy, I was insanely shocked! There were some rubbish jokes in there like: 'Why did the cow cross the road? To go and see the moo-vie!'

I was so unimpressed that I wanted someone to get her off the stage but the audience seemed to love her.

It came to the end of the act and it was time to vote yes or no. David said yes, Amanda said yes, Alesha said yes and finally, it was my turn to vote. This was a tough choice. I could either go out of my mind and say yes or say no and maybe lose my reputation as a judge.

After a few minutes, I made up my mind and had to say yes. Once I'd said yes, the crowd went crazy! Luckily, the show was finished and then I had a warm bath and lasagne.

The time is now 10.27pm and it's time to go to bed.

Night-night Diary,

Simon.

## Owen Sherlock-Scougall (9)
Dymchurch Primary School, Romney Marsh

# Penny's Adventure

Dear Diary,

I am Penny. I was in this metal box. When I got home, I was going to beg my humans to let me outside but the annoying thing was that they wouldn't let me out! I had just moved to a place, something starting with 'D', but before you forget, I am a cat.

While this was going on, I was getting really, really annoyed sitting in this cube thing. I started to need a number two.

Finally, we were there. My human opened the cube thing. I left a nice surprise in the cube thing. While my human opened it, I ran upstairs. The window was open! I ran outside, I was excited to see the other cats that live around the area.

I arrived at a place beginning with the letters 'P' 'L' and 'Z', I decided to go in to have a look around. I came across a black and white animal. He told me that he was a lemur called Larry and I was in a place called Port Lympne Zoo! I had a great chat with him for a bit and then I headed off in the direction I needed to go.

A few pawprints down, I found a cheetah called Izzy. Izzy showed me around the zoo and told me about the animals and the funny things they get up to.

I started to miss my human and decided to head back to my new home so I said goodbye to Izzy and Larry and all the animals in the zoo.

I finally found my way home to my human, I snuck through the window and lay on my human's comfy bed when all of a sudden, I heard her fuss me. I had really missed her and was glad to be back home. I think next time I decide to have a look around outside, I'll stay closer to home, but I will go and visit Izzy and Larry again!

Night Diary, it has been a hectic week!

## Phoebe Grace Tipler (9)

Dymchurch Primary School, Romney Marsh

# The War Times

Dear Diary,

This was the day, the most heartbreaking day of the war. I woke up and heard the most deafening sound of all sounds. I looked out my window and saw a bomb with smoke coming out, so I had to evacuate. I went to the village hall.

A lady came up to me said, "You're clean, you're the one I want."

She took me to the rainy countryside. We went inside. A massive, great hound tackled me like I was a toy!

"Sit boy!" shouted the lady.

I asked, "What's your name?"

"I'm Kimey," she said as I continued to just stand there.

"Go to bed."

I walked into an amazing bedroom and smiled immediately. I lay in my kingsize bed and I pulled my fluffy cover over me, then rested my head on the grand pillow and looked at all the expensive toys I had. I closed my eyes and drifted off to sleep.

In the morning, I heard no bombs at all. Kimey came into my room and said,
"Pack your toys, take what you want."
Then she walked away. I packed all my stuff and got ready.
I was happy because my mum was outside the door! The great hound was hungry so I fed him, then I said goodbye.
"Mum!" I shouted.
We hugged each other and went home.
I will write back later,
Maisie.

## Maisie Munnings (9)
Dymchurch Primary School, Romney Marsh

# The Raft Escape

Dear Diary,

I was stuck on a raft looking for land with my friend, Owen. We were fishing until we saw a volcano island so we went and looked around for fruit and vegetables. When we were stuck on the raft, we could only eat fish. At last, we had some other food. I cut trees down and Owen picked fruit. We didn't realise that the volcano was steaming up...

We finished making a house, we made a bed out of leaves, then we went exploring. The ground started to shake, then a landslide hit Owen. The ground was steaming, lava was blasting out of the volcano! Owen and I ran back to the raft, the lava burning the forest. We sailed on and on and kept on fishing. When we had a fish, we saw an island with no volcano and a city!

## Mario Skinner (8)

Dymchurch Primary School, Romney Marsh

# The Crashed Concert

Dear Diary,

My name is Jess Glynne. I had to get ready because I had a concert. I needed to look good and get a group to help me perform my song called 'Thursday'. I went to town to get an outfit and to get my friends to help me at the concert. My friends are: Katy Perry, Bruno Mars, Jonas Blue and Chainsmokers.

I got my outfit, now I needed to get their outfits. Jonas Blue said he wanted to get lunch, everyone got bacon and eggs.

After, we booked in for the show and we got dressed and had dinner. We did our thing and went on stage. Everyone was getting my autograph but one boy wanted to do a prank and got on the stage! I was shocked to see someone on the stage!

## Xin-Ling Liang (8)

Dymchurch Primary School, Romney Marsh

# The Incredible Diary Of... Katy Perry

Dear Diary,

When I was a singer, the first time I was asked to go on stage I was bursting with excitement. I was going on a tour to meet Lacey Sadler in Year 3 so I told my manager I would do it another day.

The next day, I was on the plane waiting to get to Dymchurch Primary School.

When I got there, I was really excited to tell Lacey that I wanted her to come on the tour with me. I opened the door, she looked like she was about to burst! I called out her name and she just fainted right in front of me. I felt nervous. I went to see her at the doctor's. I said it to her again so we went back to my house and we had lots of laughs.

## Lacey Sadler-Button (7)

Dymchurch Primary School, Romney Marsh

# The Incredible Diary Of... Meeting The Dangerous Shark

Dear Diary,

I was on a boat and put snorkels on and a swimming suit. I went into the sea and saw a shark! I was scared and frightened. I was shaking so I got on the boat and went home.

I played with my toys and went to bed.

The next day, I went to the beach and had some ice cream.

## Darcy (7)

Dymchurch Primary School, Romney Marsh

# The Incredible Diary Of... Safiya

Dear Diary,

So, let me explain the day that changed my life...
I woke up in the morning, got ready for school and took my matching monkey plate, cutlery and cup out of the cupboard like I always do. Everything was normal. The only thing I did differently was slice bananas and put them on top of my two waffles with chocolate spread on. Then I did my hair in a low side ponytail and put on my favourite scrunchie which has tiny little cats on it. The last thing I did was put colourful ice cubes in my water and went to feed my cat, Merlin McFlurry.

Now here's the strange part, he wasn't waiting by his food bowl for me to feed him, or in his hammock, or by the windowsill to see me go to school. Strange, right? So I just thought he went out through the cat flap.

Now it was half-past three. I was thinking about Merlin McFlurry during a teambuilding lesson but telltale Fleur Hallow said that I wasn't helping, how rude! I was holding the book open the whole time! This is the bit that changed my life... As soon as I opened the house door, I kicked my shoes off and ran into the kitchen to make some juice.

Suddenly, something brushed past my ankles and then the cat flap slammed shut. I flung open the door and was blinded for a few seconds whilst my eyes adjusted. Merlin was up in the sky! He did a loop-the-loop, leaving a trail of rainbows. He even had a unicorn horn and wings! I caught all this on camera. If I hadn't, no one would have believed me!

I showed the footage to my neighbour, who is a weatherman, he must have told his manager as the company have invited me for an interview. Of course, Merlin McFurry is coming too.

From a happy Safiya.

## Safiya Muddun (11)
High Firs Primary School, Swanley

# The Incredible Diary Of... Gregory

Dear Diary,

I was on an aeroplane from England to Tobago. It was stifling.

When I arrived in Tobago, it was the hottest place! My grandparents picked me up from the airport and showed me to a taxi. I sat in the back. I was squashed between my grandparents.

When I saw the house, I asked my grandparents, "Is this your house?"

It looked like it could fall down any second! Granny said it was. We got out of the taxi and made our way into the house.

My grandparents showed me to my room and kissed me. In my room, there was a green, slimy lizard staring at me from the ceiling. I slept very quickly because I was so tired.

In the morning, I saw a person I'd never met before. He is my cousin. His name is Lenox. Granny cooked saltfish for breakfast. I didn't like it so I spat it out. Granny looked angry, I felt bad. Granny told Lenox to show me around the house.

When we went to see the garden, I was hot and thirsty. Lenox asked me if I wanted to dip my feet in the river, I said no because I was so bored! Lenox ran to dip his feet though. I sat under a tree and played my video game.

Lenox came over. I let him play my game, he did it all wrong! Then Grandpa said he was going to have a sea bath. Lenox started cartwheeling whilst I walked all the way to the beach.

When we got there, I started swimming. Then I saw something... It was a shark! I quickly swam to shore. I felt scared. My grandparents and Lenox started laughing.

Lenox said, "They are dolphins!"

Then I started swimming with the dolphins. Lenox joined in.

Now we're going to England, I'm excited!

Gregory.

## Veda Trivedi (7)

High Firs Primary School, Swanley

# The Default

Dear Diary,

Today was the best day of my short life! I got my first Victory Royale! I dropped into Tilted Towers for the first time ever, it was amazing! All I could see were shots left, right and centre. I went inside, trembling on my toes, looking for a weapon to protect myself. I found an M16. Finally, I could attack.

Getting as much material as I could, I stepped into action. Somebody was scoping in on me, it was a heavy sniper. Not knowing what to do, I built a ceiling and luckily, he shot that. I was scared out of my mind! I started hitting my shots but then, I hit a godly headshot. He was down and out.

"Yes!" I triumphantly shouted as I went over to see his loot. "Oh, this will do the job!"

Now I was in the top ten with some very spectacular guns and weapons.

As I was running at top speed, I was stopped and started to shudder. I saw a huge fight. I didn't know how I was going to win this!

Under pressure, I was in the top five. I got in a bush and started camping. As the footsteps kept on thumping and the guns kept on shooting, I still kept my nerves.

Last guy! Now I was engaging in combat. I got up and shot my RPG, it was like an eagle eyeing its prey. It whizzed through the air and *bang!* I had won! What a day!

**Liam James Gardner (11)**
High Firs Primary School, Swanley

# The Incredible Diary Of... Mia

*An extract*

Dear Diary,
My name's Mia and I love mystical creatures...
Something happened to me today, I suddenly woke up in a huge forest full of different things like trees, leaves and lots of vines. I wondered where I was and why I was there, but I thought it would just be a new adventure. Suddenly, I heard a noise coming from the bushes. I got scared that somebody was going to attack me. I was terrified! I slowly backed away, hoping that I wouldn't get hurt, but I was too scared to wait so I ran for my life.
I was pleased I was safe again. I found a lake. I looked at my reflection. I was so surprised, I had wings, real wings! I couldn't believe my eyes. I was so happy. Then I saw two elves heading to the palace of Scentopia. I said hello to them, they told me their names, Moe and Ukeo. There were so many unicorns around the barrier! I saw dead trees on the farmlands near the palace. The elves tried to heal them but it took too much power.
Later, I went to the waterfall and the beautiful lakes to see the Northern Lights at midnight. Suddenly, my bracelet started glowing so I pushed it and I disappeared in a flash of light!

I ended up back in my room with the book Scentopia's Legends.

## Micah Weekes (8)
High Firs Primary School, Swanley

# The Space Adventure

Dear Diary,

This week, I got a goldish kind of envelope through my door so I opened it and inside was what I had been waiting for my whole life! That was my day! Well, and Hazel's of course, she had been wanting to go to space too.

I was so excited to lift off to space for five days. First we would go to Mars, then after we would go to Uranus, then we would have to go home, but that's okay. Getting a spacesuit on was really hard and actually trying to climb up all the stairs to get to the rocket was even harder.

When we arrived on Mars, Hazel was so delighted she pushed me out of the way to get out first. We were so amazed at how red and orange the planet was. Out of nowhere appeared a green, blobby character bouncing up and down. It came towards me and started to make funny noises.

Later that day, we were friends with the blob of slime and we decided to take him home with us. Three days later, we decided to go to Uranus. When we arrived, we hopped on our moon buggy and set off. I got all sorts of souvenirs!

When we got back home, me and Hazel told everyone about our space mission and about what we did. And that is the end of our week!

## Sophie Cathryn Collett (11)
High Firs Primary School, Swanley

# The Incredible Diary Of... Arthur And The Golden Rope

Dear Diary,

Today was tiring because I was sent out on a terrifying mission to save our town from a ferocious wolf named Fenrir. Some people wanted me to go on the voyage to find the god of thunder, Thor, but some people didn't think I should go at all. They said I was a meddler!

Last night, I was wondering if I should go on the voyage or not. Eventually, I decided to go on the voyage, so I snuck out of my bedroom to the harbour and I found a boat. I slowly but carefully climbed into it.

After I'd climbed into the boat, I sailed across the sea to find Thor, but suddenly, an enormous pirate ship was coming from the distance. I was worried because the pirates had swords. Luckily, I had my staff so I could fight the mighty pirates, so I carried on with my journey.

While I was carrying on with my journey, I met a huge Kraken. I tried to freeze it with the hand of time, however, it didn't work. I whacked my staff on the Kraken. Yay, it worked! That was epic! It broke all of the Kraken's bones. Suddenly, it plunged into the darkness of the deep blue sea.

I didn't think it would work, but it did!
Arthur.

## Taylor Summer Coombs (7)
High Firs Primary School, Swanley

# The Incredible Diary Of... Willy Wonka

Dear Diary,

Today was the day that I started to work in my chocolate factory. I had my Oompa-Loompas to help me make chocolate. I chose ten people to visit the factory, but the ten people were kids only. I made a newspaper to tell everyone that I'd chosen ten kids to visit my factory.

I was making some chocolate but then my chocolate machine broke! Thanks to my Oompa-Loompas, it is fixed. Then I tested the machine and it worked perfectly. I checked, there were only thirteen more hours until the ten kids came.

Finally, the kids came. I was very pleased because I'd already made a thousand chocolates! The ten kids were named: Charlie, James, Violet, Augustus Gloop, Perrie, Jack, Annie, Cholan, Merlin and Morgan le Fay. I gave them all ten chocolate each. They each gave me £10.00 so I got £100 altogether! They loved it.

When the ten kids went home, my Oompa-Loompas told everyone about my chocolate so everyone spied on me!

I've sent my Oompa-Loompas away and closed down my chocolate factory.

**Akash Saravanan (8)**

High Firs Primary School, Swanley

# The Incredible Diary Of... Ronaldinho

Dear Diary,

Today I had a healthy breakfast. I had porridge with honey all over. Yummy, my favourite! I finished my breakfast and got dressed in my suit and packed my kit bag. I packed my special football boots. They are special because they make me run fast.

I arrived at Anfield. I went into the changing room and got dressed. We went on the pitch and got into our lines. They put me in defence. I said to my coach that I was a striker!

Between the match, a fan ran onto the pitch and was attacked by a steward. He was taken off the pitch.

After that, the manager brought two brilliant players on. The whistle went, we got two goals, the other team got two goals. It went through to penalties. I was nervous. We got seven goals! We won the game. My friend gave his top away. We went up the Wembley steps and had the cup. After that, the next team came up and got their medals and went back to the changing rooms.

We went to the pub and now I am home.
Ronaldinho.

## Kaiden Officer (8)

High Firs Primary School, Swanley

# The Day Billy Was Put In Goal

Dear Diary,

Before I left my house this morning, I had a really healthy breakfast of strawberry-flavoured yoghurt and some grapes. Then I had some Rice Krispies but without sugar because sugar is not healthy.

As soon as I arrived at Selhurst Park, I met my mates, Max Meyer and Wilfred Zaha. We went to the changing rooms and changed into our kit. When we came out, I was really nervous. We were playing the mighty Chelsea, they hadn't lost one match this season.

We jogged onto the football pitch and got into position. I always play in midfield but today they put me in goal positions. I wasn't really happy because I am not good in goal, but I tried my best. We kicked off and started. The position team got the ball and they passed the ball around us. They took a shot but I saved it! My manager was so happy with me. Unfortunately, the next shot they had, the ball flew past me and that happened again and again. I am so unhappy that I let them goals in.

Billy.

**Tommy Gray (8)**
High Firs Primary School, Swanley

# The Hust Invasion

Dear Diary,

I, Jonsey, got woken up at what seemed to be night by Ray.

"Commander, wake up! We need you to eliminate these husks, we think there might be a smasher!"

So I got out of bed, got my weapons and went to battle.

As soon as I opened the door, I got smacked in the face! I disliked this so we had a slap fight and I won, obviously. Unfortunately, my roommate got attacked so I came to the rescue and eliminated all the husks, then helped him.

"You're gonna be fine. Stay here and heal," I said to him.

But then out of nowhere, a smasher!

"I'm gonna destroy this island bit by bit!"

It was launching itself into our home base, destroying everything in its path. We were swinging our swords but it wasn't doing much.

"Ha ha, you can't hurt me!"

But just then, when it laughed, I saw its weak spot and launched for it...

We defeated it. Today was crazy!

## Brandon Leslie Stephen Fraser (11)
High Firs Primary School, Swanley

# The Worst Birthday Ever

Dear Diary,

Today I woke up with a jolt, realising that today was my birthday. This was a special birthday for me because I became a decade old.

It was midday when we arrived at the ski slopes. I had never been skiing before so I had to have lessons with my mate, Mike, before we hit the slopes.

Finally, after two or three hours of the basic training, we went to a slope where I let Mike go first, who slid down gracefully. Once Mike was at the bottom, I was feeling a little more confident. I began to slide down at an amazing pace, smiling, not realising I was about to lose control and face-plant straight into the snow! I made a crunch as I hit the snow and snapped a ski, which made me feel so guilty.

In the end, I had to show Mum the damage I had done to the ski. Even though it was my birthday, Mum still made me pay, leading to my conclusion that skiing is my least favourite sport. Now I have almost no money left!

## Yuri Ayukegba (10)

High Firs Primary School, Swanley

# The Incredible Diary Of... A Unicorn

Dear Diary,

I am happy today because I've saved a life again. I really like saving lives. I feel brave and so mighty that I can save people. People have started liking me because I save lives.

I saw a pirate ship with someone trapped on it. I said, "Stop! Leave her alone!"

I went over there and used my magic horn. I climbed onto the boat but one pirate jumped off the boat. I didn't know what to do! I couldn't use my unicorn horn again, I needed to find something to fight with. I had a flying axe, I could've flown over and killed him but he was still in the water, maybe hiding under the water. Then he jumped up onto the pirate ship again! I needed to get him. Then I remembered I had brought a gun so I could shoot him far away... I got him. Now I needed to get out of there. I untied the trapped person, I used my magic powers to bring a boat and I travelled away on my little boat.

**Jessica Almeida (8)**
High Firs Primary School, Swanley

# The Day I Got A Victory Royale

Dear Diary,

Today I got my first Victory Royale! It started off as a normal game. I landed at Lucky Landing, as you can guess, it is lucky for me. All my good games are when I land there.

Eighty guys left and all I had was a green AR, a grey TAC, a grey SMG and six minis.

Seventy guys left and finally, my loot upgraded to a SCAR, a legendary pump and a P90.

Thirty guys left.

"Could this really be my game?" I said to myself. With the same loot, I got five kills!

Fifteen left, I was concentrating so hard with seven kills down to last me and two other players. In the kill feed, I saw Lukas2008R had been eliminated. A guy peeked, I hit a seventy-two headshot on him, then another seventy-two headshot. And he was dead. On my screen it said: '#1 Victory Royale!' I was so happy. I returned to the lobby and had the winner umbrella.

## Owen David D'Arcy (11)

High Firs Primary School, Swanley

# The Incredible Diary Of... Gregory

Dear Diary,

Yesterday I came to my grandparents' house in Tobago. I got on the plane. The plane was so full of people I didn't think it would take off!

I got off the plane and climbed into a taxi. I was squished between my grandparents. I was scolding hot and really exhausted.

When I arrived at my grandparents' house, I didn't expect the house to be so small. When I got to my room, it was so small, there was no TV or Xbox and there was a lizard above my head!

Grandma said, "It's time for dinner, Gregory!"

It was saltfish, yuck!

I went to bed hungry. All I could see was the lizard above my head and hear my tummy rumbling.

Now I have woken up, I have a bite on my arm from a little bug. I wonder what I am going to do today...

See you later Diary, I am going to find out!

## Daisy-May Land Goode (8)
High Firs Primary School, Swanley

# The Incredible Diary Of... Arthur And The Golden Rope

Dear Diary,

Today has been a hard day, don't you think? I found some magical worms but suddenly, I heard a howl! I rushed to the village and saw a big wolf knocking over the great fire. Everybody was freezing to death. Atrix told the whole town somebody needed to go and tell Thor to light our fire. "I can do it."

"No, not him. He's too small. He'll be ignored like us."

"No, I won't! You'll see."

So I travelled long and far. I saw a pirate ship and a sea monster nearly destroyed my boat.

I met Thor.

I said to him, "Can you light our fire?"

He said, "Yes, but you must catch the beasts."

I found a forest. There were a lot of beasts around me. I ran really fast but they still caught up with me!

## Kyla Tatou (7)

High Firs Primary School, Swanley

# The Incredible Diary Of... Cyan

Dear Diary,

Hey, it's me, Cyan, again. Why do people bully me about my name, saying it's a colour? Yeah, I know it is but I've had these sort of comments all my life and they just need to stop. I feel useless sitting here on my bed. I wish something good would happen. But instead of obsessing over what people thinking of me, I'll love my name! I like not following the crowd but it's hard to not feel hurt when you're being left out. Maybe drinking some mint chocolate milk will help. Sometimes I feel that my pen and paper are my only friends, but I suppose life is just like that so I will just drink my mint chocolate milk and check-in later (and probably doodle).

Peace,

Cyan.

## Lucy Cattermole (11)
High Firs Primary School, Swanley

# Peace!

Dear Diary,

Peace? Peace? Peace? Sorry, my little sister is driving me up the wall! Not literally, she doesn't have a driving license, but still. Anyways, right now, I'm trying to find my headphones. *Crash!* I told you she's a pain, she's smashed another plate!

Right now I'd do anything for a bit of peace and quiet. That isn't much to ask for, right? When my mum comes home in half an hour, she'll get in trouble.

Mum must be late home and my annoying sister is banging on my door... Yes! Mum's back... Oh great, no she isn't. I might have to stop writing for a bit so I don't have to tear you in half! Argh! Where is my peace?

## Jalena Li-Hutchins (10)

High Firs Primary School, Swanley

# The Incredible Diary Of... Arthur And The Golden Rope

Dear Diary,

It was really strange today. I was looking for magical worms when suddenly, I was plunged into darkness as a huge wolf jumped over me. The wolf ran back to the town and he was knocking over the houses. The wolf knocked over the great fire. Atrix began to speak.

She said, "There is a mighty warrior across the sea. Who will go? Everyone has been injured!"

But I wasn't injured so I could go. Some people said mean things to me, like that I am too small to see a mighty warrior. The townsfolk called me a meddler! I felt upset when they called me that. I told Atrix what the mean people said to me!

## Laila Tatou (7)

High Firs Primary School, Swanley

# The Incredible Diary Of... Me

Dear Diary,
I frantically tried to usher my parents to stop chatting as my favourite scene from 'Star Wars' was coming up. My mother and father asked me if I wanted some popcorn.

Delighted, I answered, "Give me loads Mum, loads!"

My mum gave me a stern look and I added solemnly, "Please."

My parents both went into the kitchen, I tensed up. The Battle of Endor was commencing! Then something utterly weird happened. Wafting out of the TV were dark and ghostly arms and before I could scream, the arms grabbed me and dragged me in!

As my weary eyes adjusted to the light, I realised, to my shock, that I was in a vast rocket! The engines were roaring like a distressed dog. The din was horrendous. Just then, a strange creature walked proudly up to me. He had a long, green face with huge, bulgy eyes as wide as tennis balls! His skin was slimy and sticky like a frog's. The alien was well aged and every minute or two, a sharp cough would spurt out his gaping mouth.

"Hello my fellow pilot, are you all set up for the dogfight of your lifetime?" he exclaimed.

I was quite taken aback by this and after a while, I replied, "Who are you and what do you mean by dogfight?"

The alien laughed a great booming laugh that echoed around the ship like a cave.

"I am Admiral Ackbar and as for the dogfight, you're going to try and blow up the Death Star and a couple of starfighters with it! May the force be with you."

As soon as we got out of the hanger, multiple objects came up on the radar. As the objects came into view, I realised that there were actually thousands upon thousands of pristine ships attacking me!

I fired two plasma bolts and one of the freighters erupted into a ball of crimson flames. I continued this annihilation until my whole brave fleet dived into the belly of the Death Star.

## Henry Kimber (9)
Hilden Oaks School, Tonbridge

# The Incredible Diary Of...

3rd April, 2089
AM
Dear Diary,
Today I am going on holiday. I am super excited because this is my first holiday in space since 2069 and because I am going to meet my new granddaughter, who is two years old already!

3rd April, 2089
PM
Dear Diary,
I strapped myself into the seat and waited for take-off. I could see all the tall, rusty structures that held the aircraft whilst it landed. Suddenly, the space shuttle lurched forward and a flurry of excited chatter erupted. I gripped the arms of my chair and hoped for the best, I've always been nervous when flying!

4th April, 2089
AM
Dear Diary,
Cautiously, I peeked out the window and saw a beautiful sunset. It was breathtakingly pretty with reds and golds and pinks all mixed together. I had to make the most of it because I would not be seeing a sunset for another couple of weeks.

4th April, 2089
PM
Dear Diary,
The shuttle landed smoothly and I stepped off. I was shocked! As I turned around, my eyes widened. My daughter had warned me that her hotel had expanded massively due to an increasing number of holiday guests and that the landing port would be bigger. I didn't realise that it would be this big though! I saw at least seventy other shuttles with passengers getting on and off everywhere.
There was a large pea-green warehouse with an electric-blue sky behind it. My feeling of surprise vanished as I heard a child call out, "Granny!"
A little toddler came racing up to me and hugged my legs. I was overjoyed to meet my granddaughter for the first time! I picked her up just as my daughter came running up to greet me too. They drove me back to their apartment (on a hover golf buggy) so I could say hello to my ten-year-old grandson and my daughter's husband.

## Izzie Denney (10)
Hilden Oaks School, Tonbridge

# The Incredible Diary Of... The Karaoke Party

Dear Diary,

You'll never believe the amazing night I had yesterday. The fun began in the evening at seven o'clock. It was karaoke night at Eileen's house. Eileen is Florence's nana. Florence is my favourite stepsister. My only stepsister. We were celebrating Eileen's birthday. All her family were there.

When we arrived, I froze. I suddenly didn't want to sing all by myself. I felt apprehensive. Although I know Florence's family, I still don't feel completely comfortable around them. They are all so friendly towards me and have welcomed Mummy, Lily and I into their family (which everybody seems to think is quite remarkable as they are Florence's mum's family and Mummy is with Florence's dad). I needed support for the first song so I sang in a group with Lily, Mummy and Florence. We chose Abba - 'The Winner Takes It All'. Everybody loved it. In fact, most of them joined in. It was a definite hit and it felt incredible. I was filled with confidence. That wasn't the only positive thing, the food was officially to die for! There was a buffet. Everyone had brought a different dish with them.

We had made hedgehogs out of fruit and one of cheese and sausages, which were extraordinary and incredibly popular!
As the evening went on, I became much more comfortable. I sang more songs with Mummy, they were brilliant. Next time, I'll go for a solo!

## Olivia Parry (10)

Hilden Oaks School, Tonbridge

# The Incredible Diary Of...
# Castlehurst Caves

Dear Diary,

I went to Castlehurst Caves today on a school trip. It was pitch-black so the teacher gave me a lantern. I dropped back to look at the old beds but when I looked back, my class was gone! I decided I would go to the left side because it seemed lighter that way. If I got lost in the dark and creepy tunnels, I would never find my way out. I carried on down the tunnel until I found the light, but it wasn't daylight or lantern light, they were spotlights. A tall, broad man was leaning over a massive bomb with springs under it. As soon as he saw me, he ordered his servant to grab hold of me. The servant seized my arm and dragged me towards the man. The man raised his hand and punched me hard in the temples.

I woke up in the corner of the cave and saw the man tapping a few buttons. He was about to launch the monumental bomb!

"Soon, the world will be mine with my hypnotising gas!"

I got up and charged at the man's stomach. He grunted. He fell back, stunned. When I had the chance, I grabbed a piece of rope I had spotted and wrapped it around the man's legs.

He wriggled to try and get free but the ropes wouldn't budge. He was like a cheetah in a boa constrictor. I ran back to where the main path was and saw my class searching for me.
"Here he is!" my friend, Fred, shouted.
From that day, the evil scientist was jailed.

## Oliver Chambers (10)
Hilden Oaks School, Tonbridge

# The Incredible Diary Of... Wilbur Wright

Dear Diary,

Yesterday, me and my brother did something incredible. It was like a miracle! We displayed a twelve-second flight. It was an extraordinary breakthrough in history. It was a pristine day for flying, one we had been looking forward to as much as receiving gold. We clambered into our dinky, old plane, which we had been making for decades. It had wings as long as a plank of wood and it was as aerodynamic as a graceful bird. For twelve exhilarating seconds, we were completing the impossible. Our plane was singing. It soared and cut the cloudless sky. All those decades of planning were dancing beautifully in front of the five fabulous spectators watching our milestone. Obviously, midflight, we hit a devastating gust of wind, whirling our poor plane down to the sandy beach. It disintegrated into shards of dreams. Before the fantastic flight, we were petrified something catastrophic would occur. At least it wasn't that bad.

We had a great time in the sky. We are incredibly proud of our achievement. Thankfully, this pioneering adventure was successful.

Next time, we are looking to fill the glass to the top by improving. With us, the glass is always half full. Next, we will complete the treacherous journey of crossing the Atlantic Ocean. We are both proud of storming the skies.

Over and out,

Wilbur Wright.

## Zak Gandhi (10)

Hilden Oaks School, Tonbridge

# The Incredible Diary Of... Me!

Dear Diary,

I just woke up and it was Wednesday. This was my favourite day because we have sport and that's my favourite thing about school.

I got dressed and went downstairs for breakfast. For breakfast, I had jam on toast, which is delicious all the time. We jumped into the car and went to school.

At school, the first lesson I had was maths with Mrs Carten, she is so strict! I had break and then English, where I struggled to concentrate. English is really challenging. I don't know how but I managed to sit through it, then it was lunch. I had a roast, it's always made beautifully by the lovely Mrs Martin. After lunch, I had a kickabout with a few of my friends because we had a football match after lunch.

After football with my friends, lunchtime was over. We got packed up and went for our match to Hilden Town, who were the opposition. On the way, everybody was screaming and shouting with excitement. I felt nervous but at the same time, happy.

As we arrived at Hilden Town, my heart was pounding like a drum. As soon as my feet touched the ball, I came alive.

After fifteen minutes, the score was 1-1 and we were heading for a draw. They defended really well until there were five minutes remaining. I shot.

Goal! I had just scored an amazing goal that won it for us!

## Samuel Museka (9)

Hilden Oaks School, Tonbridge

# The Incredible Diary Of... Rugby Ralph

Dear Diary,

Today has been a very exciting day. My dad and I watched the rugby together this afternoon. It was England vs Scotland. I had been looking forward to this match all day. At the start of the game, I felt sad because I wasn't there watching the players live or better still, playing with my favourite team. I closed my eyes and wished and wished that I could be there at Twickenham.

When I opened my eyes, I was shocked because I was at the match! Not only was I at the match, I was *playing!* Rugby Ralph strikes again! I started the match with the ball in my possession. I saw someone from Scotland running towards me, he was big and scary. He looked like a wide, furry bear hurtling towards me. But there was no time to be scared. I might be small but I am quick. I ran through his legs. I could see the try line in the distance but there were two other players in the way. I ran towards them both as they ran screaming and shouting my name. I looked around me and saw my teammates. Everything was blurred and fuzzy. Sweat dripped down my face as I dived for the line and scored a try. The crowd roared and my heart was racing.

This was the best day ever! My teammates threw me into the air to celebrate.
I had better go now as it is bedtime and I am so tired.
Ralph.

## Harry Woodward (10)
Hilden Oaks School, Tonbridge

# The Incredible Diary Of... A Young Queen

Dear Diary,

Today was a ceremonious day. I have been crowned queen of the entire Egyptian nation. I was quivering, shaking non-stop through my whole body. When I entered the hall, I thought, *this is my big moment*. I took proud, regal strides, ready for my coronation.

After the coronation, we celebrated. I wore a beautifully crafted dress, which my mother used to wear, made of leopard skin. My sandals were decorated with small sapphire jewels. I felt amazing, but at the same time, a wave of anguish flowed down my spine and I shivered. All these questions bolted to my head, *what if we have to go to war? What if I don't treat my people correctly? What if I'm too young and lose hope?* I couldn't stop thinking about it.

As the eventful day ended and the day was cracking into night, I plummeted into bed, feeling distressed. My servant came to me with my favourite Egyptian delicacy - locusts dipped in honey. I thanked her.

Being queen is an amazing feeling and maybe I shouldn't be worried about it. I am still young, right? So here I am, Cleopard VIII of Egypt, a young queen who will lead us to eminence and triumph.

**Natasha Kibara (10)**
Hilden Oaks School, Tonbridge

# Different

Dear Diary,

The first day was like any other appalling day. Yet again, Abi Woods was bullying me. Anyway, I was practising my mountain climbing.

I said to my instructor, "I want to climb Mount Everest."

He answered, "Elanor, you will never be able to climb Mount Everest because you haven't got what it takes!"

That night, I went home in floods of tears. I couldn't stop them dripping down my cheeks. But then I realised I was the bigger person. I lifted my head, wiped away my tears, stood up tall and said, "Let's do this."

I put my gear on and headed out for victory.

I was halfway there, I already had blisters, but it was warm under my big jacket and fluffy boots. The snow and ice glittered in the moonlight. I was on my fourth day and I still felt fresh, it had been a tough climb and every step became a struggle as I got closer to the summit.

At last, I was at the peak of Mount Everest. I was so pleased with myself, I couldn't stop smiling!

I was interviewed and proclaimed, "Just because some people are different, it doesn't mean they can't do amazing things. I am albino and proud!"

## Sasha Moran (10)
Hilden Oaks School, Tonbridge

# Changing America's President

Dear Diary,

Today I did something that changed history. I was just casually walking down the road when I spotted something in an alleyway. It had flashing red lights on top that said: *Time Machine.*

"Perfect," I said as I crept inside.

I typed in the coordinates and hit the big, green button that said 'Go'. I slithered out like a snake onto the White House and a big, metal duct caught my attention. I thought I could climb down it and get inside. I jumped in and as my feet touched the metal, I heard echoes surround me. Two minutes later, I was in the control room, in front of the master computer, when suddenly, I heard banging on the door. I was panicking so I quickly put my fingers on the screen and switched the Donald Trump and Hillary Clinton photos. I saw a door at the back of the room and rushed through it.

It was election time and I was sitting in the back of the crowd.

That's when they announced, "Hillary Clinton is our new president!"

I got up from my chair and shouted, "In your face, Donald Trump!"
He looked at me, staring furiously and shouted, "Go after that girl!"

## Bruna Maggie McNichol (10)

Hilden Oaks School, Tonbridge

# The Incredible Diary Of... Paul Pogba

Dear Diary,

A drop of sweat rolled down my face. This was a big game and if I didn't impress my manager, I would lose his trust and not play in the next game. As we walked through the tunnel, my friend, Anthony Martial, noticed my nerves and said, "Don't worry, you'll do great!"

"Let's do this," I said to myself.

When the game started, I was already with the ball. I did a nice one-two with Anthony and I was in brilliant space. I glanced at the goal, then blasted the ball into the top corner. Me and Anthony showed off our new celebration and with a smile, he said, "What a goal!"

As we got back into position, I said to everyone, "Stay focused!"

The opposition was ready to get back at us but our team was solid in defence. Nemanja Matic got the ball back and passed to Luke Shaw, whose cross hit an opposition arm. Penalty! I put the ball on the spot and struck the ball into the corner. In the second half, I had the ball. I spotted Anthony's run, passed to him and he slotted it past the goalkeeper.

The referee blew his whistle and we celebrated the victory together.

## Ike Young (10)
Hilden Oaks School, Tonbridge

# The Incredible Diary Of... A Robot

Dear Diary,

You will not believe what happened today! I was just going about my normal life, exploring the rocks when I heard it... *Crash!* I scanned the area and saw the most peculiar thing - a rocket-type object. I was intrigued so I went over to investigate it. I could not see very clearly because of the smoke but I saw a dark figure in a tin suit walking towards me. Using my rocket launchers, I sped away at full power, it could jump as high as a frog! I stood there in awe. I was gobsmacked!

Then I heard a deep voice say, "A robot!"

Was this creature referring to me? I looked around, I was the only one there. It was getting closer. That's when I realised it was... a human! We had alien visitors! They were real. I was speechless. It was the best day ever. He showed me to his spaceship and I showed him our planet and the moon. It was brilliant to see how amazed he was. Before he left, he gave me something. It was a photo of me and him. I will forever treasure it. R5Jim.

PS He gave me the 'Jim' part.

**Jessica Robbens (10)**
Hilden Oaks School, Tonbridge

**60**

# The Incredible Diary Of...

Dear Diary,

Today, my parents had an exciting surprise for us... We were going to the beach!

The delicious, mouth-watering food was in the steaming car, which melted my body. As we got closer to Dymchurch, Daddy realised he had turned into the middle of nowhere. Luckily the satnav pointed him in the right direction.

When we arrived at the beach, I could hear the waves crashing against the smooth sand. The tide was too far in to start to play, so we went and explored the local area.

When we had finished, we went and sat on the beach and sunbathed in sight of the bright and luminous sun.

In the afternoon we decided to go and have a paddle in the refreshing and breezy ocean. I could hear the birds squawking like a child's scream.

Later in the day, we went for a scoot around the delicious shops and went on a few rides that were a mix of exciting, scary and fun.

As the day drew to an end, we packed up and set the destination to home. I could see the sun start to set and the day drew to a close. I shut my eyes and fell asleep.

## Amber Rose Pilbeam (10)

Hilden Oaks School, Tonbridge

# The Incredible Diary Of... A Foster Child

Dear Diary,

I have lots of things I like but one of my favourite things is dragons. I used to detest dragons but now I like them and this is why...

I lived in a care institution, we had to stay indoors all the time. All I wanted was to have some fresh air so at night-time, I snuck out of my bed and went to see if the staff were awake. If they were asleep, I would tiptoe downstairs and open the door for fresh air.

Since I was still bored, I slipped down to the River Thames and dipped my toes in the water. From the banks, I saw something move as fast as a bullet in the water. Then the water started rising up in tiny splinters and there were forests of fire until all of a sudden, the river became peaceful again. There was a dragon staring at me with topaz-yellow eyes. It was silver and almost as scared of me as I was of him. I was nailed to the ground. The dragon was three elephants tall and fifteen crocodiles long from tip to toe. Suddenly, it flew into the air and was gone.

After that, I went back to sleep until morning.
When I woke up, I decided to name the dragon
Thames.
Alan Mytestone.

## Tristan Little (9)
Hilden Oaks School, Tonbridge

# The Incredible Diary Of...
# Brussels Sprouts

Dear Diary,

Today was Christmas Day. Me and my fellow Brussels sprouts were nervously waiting in a brown basket. Our months of freedom had ended and today was going to be our last day.

As me and my friendly Brussel sprouts were waiting, all of a sudden, we heard a small, fair-haired boy with dark green eyes say, "Mum, I hate Brussels sprouts and I don't want to eat them!"

"No, you *have* to eat them Ben, it's a tradition in our house!" strictly spoke a brunette lady with hazel eyes and a short bob as her hairstyle, which I assumed was the boy's mum.

I had a feeling that Ben, the little boy, may not eat us! So I told all my best friends not to go on the mum or dad's plate, just Ben's. Me, Louisa and Sarah (my best friends) jumped onto Ben's plate. Suddenly, we were bundled into a napkin and everything went pitch-black!

We jiggled around in the napkin and were thrown onto a cold, stone fireplace. Luckily, it was not lit. We looked up the chimney at the blue sky.

Standing on each other's heads, we made our escape.

## Zara Hunt (10)
Hilden Oaks School, Tonbridge

# The Incredible Diary Of... A Moody Teenager

Dear Diary,

OMG! Today was so embarrassing. Finally, an agent got me a modelling job after Mum sent my photos in three months ago. I had the address on a piece of paper but I thought, *where is Snodland?* It was hardly Paris or Milan!

On the way, I thought, *finally, someone has realised my talent!*

When I got there, it was an old warehouse. I managed to console myself by thinking, *never judge a book by its cover.* When I walked in, it was all dingy and smelly, then a lady with a clipboard walked out and said, "This way."

I walked into a changing room with the lady, she told me to put on a frilly dressing gown and a flowery shower cap. I looked at it with horror but the lady said that time was short and I had to wear it.

I walked onto the stage, it looked like an old people's home! By the end of it, I had worn a frilly dress and been on a mobility scooter. They told me it was going in the 'Grey Monthly', which is what my friends' nans read. I will never live this down!

## Laila Gibson (9)

Hilden Oaks School, Tonbridge

# Trapped

Dear Diary,

It's never easy being trapped. My cell is like the night sky without any stars. I hate being in prison! Every meal is the same - mushy green stuff that looks like bogies and smells like dog food. I guess I will just have to get used to the rock-hard bed, the horrible smell and the cramped space. There isn't even any games or entertainment, let alone friends. I've been wearing the same stinky, black and white PJs and they're starting to get sticky with sweat! My fellow prisoners aren't very nice either. Probably because they're feeling as miserable as I am.

It's freezing in the cell. It's like exploring the Arctic but forgetting to bring a coat. I hope I'm out soon!

Dear Diary,

It's a few hours later and my mum has said, "Scarlet, you can come down now, but remember, what do you say to your little brother?"

Finally, the gate to freedom has been opened and my heart has risen from the melancholy pool it was trapped in. I feel as if I could fly!

## Ava Cobb (10)
Hilden Oaks School, Tonbridge

# Water

Dear Diary,

This is me, Water. Yes, I am a water particle, don't laugh. I was in a large body of water and had a lovely wife, a salt particle called Salty. It was Tuesday.

"Morning!" a grumpy water particle grunted next to me.

I shouted, "Morning means sun and sun means warmth and warmth means evaporation!"

Every raindrop heard me and trembled. As the rays of the sun beat down on us, I couldn't believe I was going to lose my wife. I was whisked away by stinky, stanky Mrs Sun!

I hate being in a cloud, all fluffy and clingy. You think it's jolly fine when you're an air particle, but no way when you're a water particle.

Thunder rolled overhead and our cloud started to move in a northeast direction. The cloud deposited us and as we fell through the air, most of us promptly fell headfirst into a muddy puddle, trust me, it isn't fun! Then we proceeded to dribble down a ditch and entered the lake, my lake. I was home, but I still had to find my wife.

## Isaac Delaney (10)
Hilden Oaks School, Tonbridge

# The Incredible Diary Of... Shackleton

Dear Diary,

My ship is currently being crushed by pack ice and my crew is ravenous. I need to make a grim journey to South Georgia to get my entire crew to safety. Panic, stress, anxiety are the only emotions I can feel right now. What if I crash and the others are stranded in Antarctica? All these questions are racing around my head but all I can do is hope and eventually try.

Dear Diary,

Today is the day. Today I have to make the treacherous journey across the North Atlantic Ocean to South Georgia (750 nautical miles). Then I have to hike over a mountain to get to a messaging point. Then, and only then, can I make the message to get my crew back to safety. I have to take it step by step. The most nervewracking part is definitely leaving most of my crew behind. But now, I have to go to Elephant Island to get my message sent. I will probably look back on today thinking how brave I was, but right now, I just hope I'll survive. Budda once said, 'We live in the moment', so I shall.

**Elodie Hodgson (10)**
Hilden Oaks School, Tonbridge

# The Incredible Diary Of... Barry Dozzie

Dear Diary,

I can't believe it... What a day I've just had! Tom and I decided to go to the local funfair. Mum and Dad let us go on our own, so that meant I could be as crazy and as silly as I liked.

The haunted house really lived up to its name. I can't remember ever feeling more scared in all my life! We both climbed into the front carriage of the train (everyone knows that's the coolest) but that turned out to be a really bad decision.

It all started off pretty normal, but then I felt something tickling me. I thought it was Tom having a laugh but then I saw it... A really pale white ghost with red flashing eyes. I swiped at it and my hand went straight through it! It wasn't just a sheet... It must have been a real ghost! I screamed and grabbed Tom and thankfully, the ride was coming to an end.

Tom couldn't stop laughing at me and thought I was joking. I can't believe he didn't see it! It was so big and real. I'm sure it wasn't just my imagination!

**Joseph Jewell (10)**
Hilden Oaks School, Tonbridge

# The Incredible Diary Of... Food

Dear Diary,

My tummy was rumbling, I was starving! I walked around school clenching my empty tummy. I reached into my pocket to get some of the leftover crumbs from break. When I reached into my pocket, I felt five boxes of Smints.

"Food!" I screamed.

I threw water over my face to check it wasn't a dream. No, it was not. I was actually holding food. I was astonished, my heart was on fire! I scoffed all of the Smints in my mouth at once. I couldn't wait any longer. My mouth was trembling with fire as it seemed it was as hot as a volcano. I ran screaming as loud as a lion's roar. The water fountain had a sign: *Out Of Order*. My heart was beating as fast as a crocodile's snap. I ran into the toilets with my mouth still on fire, but my legs were hovering above the old floorboards.

I shouted, "Flames, fire!"

I flew, I felt like Superman! I was flying. I crash-landed on the top of a volcano. Instead of my tummy rumbling, it was the volcano!

## Daisy Lyons (10)

Hilden Oaks School, Tonbridge

# The Incredible Diary Of... An Artist Named Emma

Dear Diary,

I am just about to have my art exam at university. I am really nervous because if I don't pass the test, I won't get an art scholarship. I really love art and I'm sure I'm very good at it, but this test is really important to me so I'm hoping I can do it. My art teacher, Mr Philips, will be our teacher for the test. He is a pro at art and I'm not nearly as good as him.

I'm only eighteen. I'm writing a diary when I'm eighteen, unbelievable! At least I can actually do art. Art is literally the only thing I'm good at. Besides English and maths, it's my best subject.

I'm going to paint a field of poppies. I have my red paint and all the other colours I need in my bag. If I pass, I suspect my mother will be very proud. After the test, when I get home, even if I pass or not, I will tell her all about the techniques I used to do my painting and I will bring home the picture.

I really hope I pass and not freak out!

Emma.

## Bianca Maxine McNichol (10)

Hilden Oaks School, Tonbridge

# The Amazing Diary Of Balthazar

Sunday 21st September, 2018

Dear Diary,

I woke up at six to go and lie on Mummy's bed. As usual, she threw me off and told me to go to bed. I untriumphantly walked to my bed and napped. About an hour later, light began to seep through. I got up onto my legs and charged into Kiki's room, onto the bed. I began to trample all over her. When the door opened, Nico came charging out and began to cuddle me. I proudly presented him his slipper, just to be told off and shooed out. I headed downstairs with revenge in mind. I sneakily edged into the kitchen and jumped, snatching the toast, then I was off into the toilet to eat in peace. An hour later, I was being bundled into the car, off on a walk. I stared at the cars going past until we arrived.

When the boot opened, I was free. I began to run and jump with joy, jumping in reverse until the car was a house away, when I saw a dog! I began to run around him when I was bundled back into the car, heading home.

**Nico Swainson (9)**

Hilden Oaks School, Tonbridge

# The Incredible Diary Of... A Sausage

Dear Diary,

Here I am, sitting in a tummy, all crunched up and squished. I'll tell you my story. Yes, just to say it, I am a sausage.

There I was lying in a packet with friends, that are sausages. One was called Bobby and the other, James. Suddenly, the packet opened. They grabbed me and flopped me on a dark, crusty pan. There was only one word to describe me - petrified! The pan got really hot, then really, really hot, then really, really, *really* hot! I was burning. Then my friends, James and Bobby, jumped on the pan and flipped it over. I fell onto the floor. The others quickly grabbed me and rinsed me under cold water. It was quite a shock. Then I was back on the boiling hot pan.

An hour later, my skin colour had changed. I was almost dead. Then I was delivered to a house in a box, a beige box. I was crunched up in a person's mouth. Swashing around like a washing machine, I can't feel my body, I sit here, waiting to be digested...

## Eaton Phillips (9)

Hilden Oaks School, Tonbridge

# A Car Crash

Dear Diary,

I am writing this in the garage. I had a big crash earlier. This is what happened...

I was driving along a country lane when a big gust of wind nearly blew me over. As I rounded the corner, I noticed a large tree had fallen onto the road. I swerved to avoid it and crashed through the crash barrier. I tumbled down the slope with wind running through my windows. The wood and metal splintered around me as I slid through the forest on my roof. It was the scariest thing that had ever happened to me. I really hoped my owner was okay.

After what felt like ages, blue, flashing lights and a pickup truck came flying down the lane. There was lots of commotion as my owner was put into the back of the ambulance. I was relieved to hear him talking to the medics. I was pulled out of the forest and finally towed to where I find myself now. The mechanics think I will be okay but I will need to be here for a few days.

## Thomas Fisher (10)
Hilden Oaks School, Tonbridge

# The Scariest Day Of My Life

Dear Diary,

Today I was scared to death. I kept seeing a figure pop up in the corner of my eye. As I finished English, I went next door because we had art. Then the loudest alarm I had ever heard went off. I realised it was the fire alarm. I ran, my best friend's face was so pale, it looked like a bedsheet. I asked him if he was okay, he didn't reply, he just ran away. Suddenly, opposite me was the figure.

He said, "Hello Jake Santos."

So I ran like lightning.

Soon, I was downstairs. I had the feeling the strange figure followed me so I kept running down the stairs until I quickly slipped into the door next to me. I heard nothing but my instinct, which was telling me to run, run and don't stop until you're outside. So I ran to the light and thought to myself, *I actually might make it out alive.* I jumped out of the window and was safe at long last.

## Thomas Hunt (10)
Hilden Oaks School, Tonbridge

# The Incredible Diary Of... Me And My Mum Tracey Beaker

Dear Diary,

At school today, I got pushed over by Tyrone. I was reading my book in the peace garden because I don't have any friends. Anyway, Tyrone came in and wasn't saying nice words. Then he got annoyed and snatched my book from me. I felt upset and decided to read the school badge on my cardigan (as if that would help) but that made Tyrone worse. He pushed me onto the floor and walked away. Scared and upset, I didn't know what to do. With a bump on my head and bleeding knees, I sat in class thinking about what to do. What had I done to make Tyrone so angry?

The end came soon enough and I hobbled over to my mum, Tracy Beaker. She asked what had happened so I told her all about it. Then my mum grabbed my hand and we rushed straight to the teacher. I was worried that my mum was going to shout at the teachers but when she came out, she was as smiley as a Cheshire cat! It made me feel happy. Everything was going to be alright.

And that was the end of the day after I was pushed over.

## Jessica Keen (8)
River Primary School, River

# Rosie River's Emotional Roller Coaster

Dear Diary,

Earlier, when I woke up this morning, I was not feeling happy because some tall, mean boys at my school were picking on me yesterday. They are called Percy Pecko and Robbie Ramsbottom. So when I went out at break today, I had no one to play with. Sitting on the freshly cut grass, I felt excited when I felt a tap on my shoulder because I thought someone was going to play with me, but it was just Percy and Robbie throwing stones at me. I almost cried. I felt relieved when the bell went and we went back to class. Not even double maths is as bad as this.

Maths came and went and before I knew it, I was back outside for lunch. In the dinner hall, things went from bad to worse. I sat nervously behind Percy and Robbie but they saw me and made fun of my prawn cocktail crisps. They made me drop the whole packet on the floor!

When I went back to class, it was PE and the boys were excited to play football, so was I. They said only boys could play football. I was determined to prove them wrong.

After the match, everyone praised me and told me how talented I was. Now everyone in the school - even Percy and Robbie - want to play with me. I can't wait to go to school tomorrow!

**Megan Mercer (8)**

River Primary School, River

YoungWriters
Est. 1991

# The Incredible Diary Of... Mike The Brave

Dear Diary,

Today my dog got sucked into a book and my cat went missing. This is how it started.

The morning started off like any other. Me and my dog were reading our favourite book 'Mike the Brave', then I got off the sofa and said to my dog, "Lenny, we should do something."

But Lenny didn't listen, he kept reading the book so I turned around and called for Dennis the cat, but he didn't come. Then I heard a loud bark. I quickly turned around. Lenny was gone! I rushed to the kitchen to find Mum and Dad, they had gone out. I saw a package on the counter: 'Magical books, a treat for cats and dogs'. I thought to myself, *what if... no, they might get sucked into the book...*

I ran to the book. They *had!* I couldn't believe my eyes! They were in the book. The one thing was they could speak and move. Suddenly, Lenny turned into Mike the Brave (the dragon), he had one big tail, a snuffy nose and wings. Then a riddle came up. I had to read the whole book! Lenny was flying Dennis all over the world: Egypt, New York, Russia, China and England.

I was so close to the end, then I finished it and now we're all back together.

## Alice Greenwood (8)
River Primary School, River

# The Story Of The Dragon

Dear Diary,

I am a kind and friendly dragon. Sadly, I live by myself, but I have a ton of caring, sweet friends so I don't mind much. I bet you can't guess where I live! I live in the weirdest place, it's actually not that bad though. Well, what you have all been waiting for is... I live in a volcano! It kind of makes sense because I breathe fire and my name is Burn. Now I need to talk to you about my friends, my amazing friends. I actually only have two but they are so generous, they'll do anything for me. We go to school together, we also play together at school, but not always, sometimes we just sit down and watch the view.

Today at school we made pizzas. It was very fun because we got to put our own toppings on. After that, we made orange juice to wash it all down. We had to put some water into a cup but not fill it to the top because we had to put some flavour thing in. Once that was finished, we had to go home so I said bye to everyone and went home.

**Lily Marshall (9)**
River Primary School, River

# The Incredible Diary Of... Krat Brothers

Dear Diary,

It's day one of living in the dense jungle of Madagascar. As it's very late, me, Martin and my younger brother, Chris, are setting up camp in the trees.

Dear Diary,

Hi, day two, rise and shine! Anyway, we're here to find an endangered creature, the clouded leopard. It gets its name from the pattern on its back.
Bye for now.

Dear Diary,

Hey, day three! Yesterday we spotted a creature moving in the trees. Today we've seen that it has disappeared completely. We've been tracking a villain called Danita Danarta and we've found that she had taken the clouded leopard. We narrowly saved the leopard but then we found out that it is female... and pregnant!

Dear Diary,

Day 63 and the female doesn't look well. We think... oh! Now we know that she was pregnant because here are the cubs!

**Eva Yarrow (9)**

River Primary School, River

# Scaring The School

Dear Diary,

Yesterday was a boring Monday! A school day, the only thing I like about school is seeing my best friend, Olivia. I always walk my puppy, Marshmellow, to school. Today she was really excited for some reason!

The first lesson that we had was maths. I'm not very good at maths. I think it's really tough. I was looking out of the window. I saw a weird, suspicious man looking through a classroom window. I turned round to Olivia, who was right next to me, and whispered, "Who is that suspicious man looking through the window?"

She replied, "I don't know."

I felt very scared, I had a million questions. How did he get into the school? Did he pretend to be someone he's not?

Next, we went to some other classes and told them what was going on.

Later, we tried to make traps to capture the evil spy. Luckily, we managed to catch him. Olivia called the police and they came as quick as they could.

We tried to save our school, we succeeded! Goodnight Diary, hope to write soon.

## Sienna Jo Burns (10)
Smarden Primary School, Smarden

# I Have To Get Out

Dear Diary,
On Monday, well, at least, that's what I thought, I woke up with a startle. I was shivering cold, freezing in fact. I was really agitated. You'll never guess why, I was somewhere, I didn't know where. Lost, that's what I was. I guessed I was in some random room.
I got out of bed and there in front of me was the incredible sight of mazes and puzzles. I realised I was isolated, then something caught my eye. A sign that said: 'Complete the puzzles and this will all be a dream!'
I started searching for an answer, I was desperate to get out of here as soon as possible.
An hour passed, I was still looking for an answer. I was now worried, scared and frightened. What if there was a set timer? I could be stuck in here forever! I got through quite a few puzzles but there were loads more...
I woke up... So it was all a dream.
I hope to write again soon with more adventures. Hopefully, I'm not going to get any more scary dreams.

## Tilda Goodwin (10)
Smarden Primary School, Smarden

# Amazing Quad Bikes

Tuesday 2nd May, 2012

Dear Diary,

Today was an excellent and awful day. It was excellent because I went on my quad bike and we built a track for it. It was pretty cool, we built a ramp. Me and my brother both have quad bikes but mine is a little bit faster. I really like the ramp because it feels like I'm flying. When I go for it, it's really cool. My brother doesn't really go on his though, he likes to watch me go on mine.

At the end of the day, the quad bike started to run out of fuel so I had to push it all of the way back to the pump to get it refuelled so I could go again. First I had to find the fuel, it took ten minutes for me to find it but I eventually found it buried at the back of the unit. After I'd put the fuel in, I had to try and start it. It worked straight away so I went back out. This is when the danger happened... I went off at 40mph and smashed my head on the ground. My quad bike fell over me, but I was okay and got back on.

## Linden Hodgkins (10)

Smarden Primary School, Smarden

# The Diary Of A Spy

Dear Diary,

I'm so mad at myself all over a job! Well, I guess you want to know what I'm talking about. It all started on Thursday when I went to Africa for my dream job. On the first day there, something awful happened. I got fired! I was so angry so I went to Evie's house to talk and guess what she gave me? A job! It turned out that I would be spying on the business that fired me! Evie said she would help me.

As we entered, I was knocked out. The next thing I knew, I was in an escape room! I saw a huge spider climb up Evie's back. Evie had been bitten! I felt a ripple of fear run down my spine as a big, purple lump appeared on Evie's neck. Suddenly, I heard a scream. As I turned, I saw a body lying on the floor. I felt isolated, I was alone. The floor had water about to go to my knees. I grabbed my gun and shot a hole through the wall. I broke it apart, I could just fit through.

Freedom!

Bye.

## Scarlett Ida Adams (9)

Smarden Primary School, Smarden

# The Competition

Dear Diary,

On Monday, I was so excited and nervous. I woke up and left by 06.45am. I was so tired, I fell asleep on the way to my competition. It was around a 1-2 hour drive, then we got there at 7.50am. As I walked in, it was massive. I stepped in and loved it, it was awesome! Me and my friends sat and waited for our competition to start. We were all excited and there were nerves rushing through our bodies. Then they called us, it was our turn. We started our warm-up, then we finished it.

Next was bars. I got 12.450, then it was the beams and I got 11.5000. After it was the floor, I did really well, I got 12.540, then R&C, which stands for 'range and conditioning'. I got 11.320. The next piece was the vault, my best and favourite piece, but then I hurt myself. I couldn't walk on it, it hurt so bad! I came eighteenth out of sixty-six people.

I hope to write back soon,

IB.

**Immy Barber (10)**
Smarden Primary School, Smarden

# The Adventure

Monday 25th March, 2019
Dear Diary,
I woke up, it was the most exciting day of my life because my friend and I were going to the jungle. We got there, it was amazing and beautiful. The trees and creatures were very dangerous. First, we built a shelter and got our things out but next to me was a very long snake. I was terrified of what might happen.
After that, we tried to get water, not food because we still had tons and tons of that in our bags. We got our water from the well that didn't really work anymore. All these creatures tried to eat me and my friend!
It was as dark as night, I was trying to sleep but all I could smell was dirt. Also, I was sleeping in very wet and dirty mud and nobody would like that. Now we've both woken up in the middle of the night and are looking out of the carpet, there are so many creatures!
I will write back if I am still alive...

## Claire Flanagan (9)
Smarden Primary School, Smarden

# The Worst Day Ever!

Dear Diary,

Yesterday was the best day of my life. My heart is still thumping at the thought of what happened yesterday. To get started, I nearly died. Okay, so where do I start?

I started off the day playing football at Wembley Stadium.

When I got home, I made a fort. I used trees, tarp and rope. Inside, I made a pillow out of twigs and leaves. Then something bad happened. A bus came flying past the fort. It looked like a school bus. Inside were zombie children! They must have been turned into zombies on their way to school! I was standing up so when the bus came past, I flew into the bush. I remembered that I had made a potion for zombies the other day. I yanked it out of my bag. I threw it at the zombies, the glass exploded and the liquid spat on the zombies. Slowly, all the zombies turned back to their human selves.

Write again tomorrow.

Goodnight Diary.

## Ebony Mansfield-Adams (10)

Smarden Primary School, Smarden

# Me And Little Mix

Dear Diary,

Today was the best ever in my life! I went shopping with my friends: Olivia, Sienna, Kari, Evie and Scarlett.

We got there and straight away went into Smiggle. We bought three pots of slime each and then decided to go to Claire's Accessories. You'll never guess who we saw in there... Little Mix! All four of them. I know, I couldn't believe it either! Olivia was the one who pointed it out, she knows everything about Little Mix. Evie nearly fainted! We all rushed up to them, I got a selfie and all of their autographs. We had a chat and thanks to me, we got their email addresses, then we actually went to Perrie Edward's house! We even saw her super cute dog. Then we played hide-and-seek. Jade made us dinner, it was so nice.

After that, we went home. Little Mix are our BFFs. I wonder if I'll meet Ariana Grande tomorrow... Write soon.

## Isla Hardwick (10)

Smarden Primary School, Smarden

# Happy Birthday

Dear Diary,

Yesterday we (meaning my mum and I) went to see West Ham in the big arena! Whilst I was watching excitedly, my mum was acting like it was more enjoyable the last time. She was nudging me every five minutes, it was really creepy!

The whistle eventually blew, I looked behind me and then back again because what I say blew my eyeballs out! My face was on the big screen and the words said: 'Happy birthday!'

I started feeling faint like I was going to fall, was this just a dream? No, it wasn't. The crowd all turned around and sang 'Happy Birthday'. It was definitely real! I ran down what seemed like a hundred steps and hugged Andy. This was the best day ever. My heart pounded like a race car. My tummy turned like a washing machine. My hair matted like a dog. OMG! He hugged me back...

This was a day I'll remember!

Write soon.

## Millie Jane Jennings (10)
Smarden Primary School, Smarden

# Almost Death

Dear Diary,
Yesterday was the toughest day of this war so far.
All horses were herded into no man's land. I ran
into barbed wire, it ripped at my leg. I hobbled all
the way to the dry beach of Dunkirk. No longer
with my best friend, Troy, by my side, I felt weak
and lonely. You are the only one I have to talk to
now. The English found me and bought me back to
their stables.
When I got back, I suffered from tetanus, also
known as lockjaw, from my wound. It was horrible
but I got better. It was said that the war had
ended, that Germany had had enough like the
English. And sure enough, an hour later, it ended. I
was called a hero but I think you know the real
hero is Troy.
I have to go and pull a farm cart now, I'll write
again tomorrow.

## Ruby Perry (10)
Smarden Primary School, Smarden

# Wrotham Village Walk

Dear Diary,

Yesterday afternoon on the 26th of March, I was filled with anticipation because we were going on a village walk around Wrotham! We had to get into groups and I was in Ella's mum's group. We had a map and we had to go in different areas of Wrotham. First, we had to go to the park. My group was Ella, Joshua, Teddy and myself, Amelie. I was so excited, I nearly fell off my chair!

When we started we walked to the park and we had to ask questions. A little while later, we came to an oak tree and its owner was Stephen Hollinshead. Meanwhile, we went to the churchyard and we had to look at a grave which had a rose on it.

On our way and before we went to Ella's house, we had to look at the objects and animals on the sign that says Wrotham. When we got to Ella's house, you will never believe this, but there was a Pinot Noir vine in her garden. We had to get all the way round Wrotham and on the way back to school I found a dead rat! The trip was so fun.

When we got back to school, we had an extra play. We kept on doing piggybacks. When the village walk was over, I was so sad!

**Amelie Rose Meynen (9)**
St George's CE Primary School, Wrotham

# Wrotham Walk

Dear Diary,

Yesterday I had been given an extraordinary chance and today I was walking on a pilgrimage. I was filled with anticipation yesterday afternoon but a bit of boredom was mixed in because of the boring work at school. I couldn't even concentrate because I kept thinking about the walk, but when Mrs Baylis announced that we would be doing the village walk, I was filled with excitement.

When my group (me, Teddy, Amelie, Ella, Alice) was announced to go and line up at the door with Mrs Finley, I jumped out of my seat, raced to the door, not even noticing what I was doing.

Just before we started our walk, we were given a quiz sheet, where we had to walk around the village of Wrotham to find the answers. *Good for exercise*, I thought. I didn't really mind if we won or lost anyway, after being told it is not a race. Still, I ran to every point with enthusiasm.

First of all, we walked down Old London Road to the play park, where we discovered when it was built and whom it was dedicated to. Afterwards, we walked (well, most of us ran) to the next place nearby nicknamed 'Noddy's Oak' dedicated to Stephen Hollinshead who died at eighteen. We carried on walking through Wrotham Village, directing and giving the answers to Mrs Finley.

I especially enjoyed giving the house names to Mrs Finley. When we were close to finishing the course I was utterly joyous that we had learnt lots. I couldn't wait for what we would trek next term.

**Joshua Lemuel Miranda (9)**
St George's CE Primary School, Wrotham

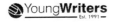

# A Village Walk

Dear Diary,

Yesterday afternoon we were reading our books. I was so excited and filled to the brim with anticipation. After a long time, Mrs Baylis announced who was going with who. We all set off and waited for Ella at her garden. Once everyone had gone to her house we set off again.

After, we had been to Ella's and played football we named all the houses along Borough Green Road. There were so many! After a while, we came to St Mary's Road which had many houses on it. Next up, we went to the butcher's shop.

A couple of minutes later, we came to the Betterson cottage which had many Roman numerals on it. It was right by the old workhouse which was for poor and puny orphans. It was on the left of Amelie's house. Next, we saw the exquisite Bull Hotel. It was so pretty. Outside there were many herbs like lovage, Greek mint, oregano, thyme and apple mint. The smells were outstanding.

After that, we came across an old plaque which was put there when Colonel Shadwell took a shot to the heart around 1799. After we looked at a few more landmarks, there was one question on the sheet. We found a cool historic landmark and set off again.

It was so funny because Teddy was pretending to be an old man. Ha! Ha! Ha!
When we got to school we were allowed to play. We jumped with joy and played 'taxis'. We chased each other into school. I marked the sheet.
I said, "My favourite part was going to the Bull Hotel."

## Alice Nuttall (9)
St George's CE Primary School, Wrotham

# Wrotham Walk

Dear Diary,
Yesterday afternoon we were filled with anticipation because we were excited about going on a village walk. We were in the classroom reading and then we were all talking about the walk. All of the parents came down to get us ready for the walk. The parents wore bright green jackets so we could see them. My team had to go first so we could get to my garden before everybody else. I said, "I can't wait to go onto the next clue!"
We started the first walk and the first clue. It was at the park on a fence on the plaque. Then everyone else caught up with us. As soon as everyone caught up we left.
After a while, we went to an oak tree, it was planted in memory of Stephen Hollinshead. The next clue was in the churchyard, it was about a flower but what one? It was a rose.
Then we did a few more clues and then went to my garden to look at the Pinot Noir vine. It was rusty, twiny, flaky and long. We played football before everyone else came. Before long I saw a dead fly on the floor and I kicked it. We then went to see the old butcher's shop and the old workhouse as well. Then we went up the road to the Clock House to see when it had been established. It was 1988.

Eventually, we got up the hill near the bins. Then we went back to school and we had ten minutes playing. We had the best day walking around the village and answering all the questions.

## Eleanor Finley (8)
St George's CE Primary School, Wrotham

# The Village Walk

Dear Diary,

Yesterday afternoon, we were filled with anticipation because we were excited about going on a village walk. My group were Tilly, Patience, Archie, William and myself. Our grown-up was Tilly's Mum, Charlie.

The first place we went to was the Wrotham sign to see what four places there were. I found one which was a warehouse. I knew I had seen it coming into Wrotham Village.

Next, we went to Ella's garden to see the Pinot Noir vine and we took a cutting off the vine. Next, we looked at the cottages to see what they were and my group got them all right. Before I knew it, we had to figure out what place was the old butcher's. I was the first one to see it, it was a really nice little cottage, it looked well used.

Next, Patience and I were looking on our own in a window that had the cutest cat called Archie. It was only three months old. It was so cute and it loved us. We felt lucky. We were the only ones in our group, well actually in my class, to see him.

Next, we went to the Bull Hotel and Patience and I looked around the place. We even looked around the back. William said, "I need a rest, I'm puffed out."

It was a lovely day, my most favourite part was going into Ella's garden and seeing the Pinot Noir vine. My second favourite part was seeing Archie the cat because I felt so lucky to see him.

## Morgan Gillham (9)
St George's CE Primary School, Wrotham

# Our Wrotham Village Walk

Dear Diary,

On the 26th of March, we went on a walk around the village (Wrotham). However, I was really enjoying my book so I did not want to leave. Eventually, we set off. We then went towards the park and we answered our first question. When was the Wrotham playpark first opened to the public? The answer was August 2015. Then we headed for the church where we answered a second question. After that, we went to our second stop and went to see the plaque of a soldier.

We walked to an antique clock shop where we had to see when the shop was established and it was 1988. Then we saw a very old-fashioned Mercedes-Benz parked by the shop.

We then went to Ella's garden where we saw the Pinot Noir vine. We crossed the road and our next quiz question was recording the names of the houses along the lane. After that, we walked to an old butcher's shop and we had to figure out the Roman numerals on the wall.

We had now done all of the stops on our map so we had to go back to school.

At school our group was very early so we had about twenty minutes playtime until the last group came back and all the volunteers had left.

**William Lambert (9)**
St George's CE Primary School, Wrotham

# The Wrotham Walk

Dear Diary,

Yesterday, which was Tuesday 26th March, we went on a village walk. I was filled with excitement and joy but it was in the afternoon. At twelve o'clock we sat at the desks doing some reading. Some people were chatting about the walk. A bit later the teacher said we were going on the village walk.

In the blink of an eye, I was out the door, in the line, waiting. As we started to go I ran ahead and stumbled and nearly fell flat on my face. I got back up and followed the class.

We walked out of the school gate and up the street we found the first place we had to write down. It was a tree and we had to write down what it said.

As we carried on walking, we found the second place which was an old antique shop. We walked down to my friend's house to look at the Pinot Noir vine, it was like a nest.

After we finished looking at it we named all the houses on that road. As we came back up we ran to the Bull Hotel and found the person who was shot in the heart in 1799 who was Colonel Shadwell.

We went back to school and waited for break.

**Archie Wilgan (9)**
St George's CE Primary School, Wrotham

# Wrotham Village

Dear Diary,

Yesterday afternoon, we were filled with anticipation because we were going on a village walk. When we saw the Pinot Noir vine in Ella's garden we all wanted a cutting. Then my group were learning so much about Wrotham and Charlie and I had a moment of silence for George Child who was shot in the heart by a deserter.

Meanwhile, our group discovered that there were Roman numerals on the old butcher's shop. Next, we found out that an oak tree was planted for Stephen Hollinshead.

After that, we were walking to the churchyard where we found a special grave. We then took a rest because we were worn out.

After a while, we couldn't find the others but we did find one group so that was good. Then we walked down Pilgrims way where I lay on the road, it was funny.

After that, Mrs Lloyd tried to ring Mrs Baylis but she didn't answer, then we just walked back to school. When we were walking back from school I saw my mum and stepdad's car and I got in it. My friends said, "That's not fair!"

## Dalyn Robertson (9)

St George's CE Primary School, Wrotham

# Wrotham Village Walk

Dear Diary,

Yesterday afternoon, we were filled with anticipation because we were going on a village walk with our friends. My group was Holly's mum, Holly, Bella, Lilly, Nicholas and me, Hillary. As we were going with the Year 3s, they were already lined up outside. When we were ready we headed out of the gates of our beautiful school.

After a while, we found an oak tree which was dedicated to Noddy and he was right in front of the oak tree. Then we jogged to the Wrotham sign and on the sign, it had a jug, horse with a lady on, past houses and the church.

Later we walked down Borough Green to go to Ella's house. When we got there we saw the Pinot Noir vine that was going to have berries on it.

After we left we found ourselves going round in a circle but as we were doing that we found a house which had Roman numerals.

After, we sadly went back to school. In the end, I sat down on the school steps and was thinking about what my mum would do on the walk. Sadly this might be my last one but it was my favourite.

**Hillary Konteng (8)**
St George's CE Primary School, Wrotham

# Wrotham Walk

Dear Diary,
Yesterday afternoon, we were filled with anticipation because we were excited about going on a village walk. We went with adults. I got picked by Holly and Lilly. The adults were: Mrs Baylis, Mrs Lloyd, Ella's mum, Ollie's mum and Holly's mum. We walked along Pilgrims Way. We were the slowest group out of the whole walk. Mrs Baylis' group had to wait for us because we took so long. We went to Ella's house and saw her Pinot Noir. It was crooked, crusty and rusty.
We went to the churchyard and tried to find a stone with holes in. There was a tree that was planted for Noddy Hollinshead. George Child was not a child but was shot in the heart. We saw an old house and it used to be an old butcher's shop. The Bull Hotel has a plaque that says a man was killed. He was an officer and was catching a criminal. There was a herb field and I ate some rosemary and some chilli plants.
We then went back to school and went home.

## Nicholas Harry Patrick Waller (8)
St George's CE Primary School, Wrotham

# Wrotham Walk

Dear Diary,

On Tuesday 26th of March we excitedly went to see all around the magnificent village. First, we strolled to see the churchyard. Next, we went to the old clock shop that was unfortunately closed. After that, we came across another shop with a cat. The cat's name was Archie and he loved me and Morgan.

After that, we went to the tasty Bull Hotel. There were some mint leaves. Archie ate one but they were rank. Then we went to the oldest shop in the village. "We found it," I yelled.

We found where George Child was stabbed in the heart and is now buried in the churchyard.

I hurt my leg and Charlie helped me by giving me a piggyback. We saw the tree planted for Noddy. We saw a house and stable and my group thought that they were linked because we found out it is his resting place.

When we got back from the village walk it was playtime for Years 3 and 4. We talked about the village walk.

## Patience Climpson (8)

St George's CE Primary School, Wrotham

# Wrotham Walk

Dear Diary,

Yesterday afternoon we were filled with anticipation and joy because we were going to walk around Wrotham. We set off on our walk. We were doing a quiz about Wrotham. The first stop was the park. We had to figure out when the park was made.

Next, we had to go to an oak tree that was planted for Stephen Hollinshead. We then went to Ella's garden which has a cold, crusty branch. After a while, we saw an old butcher's shop. Before long we were at the Bull Hotel looking at all the herbs they use.

After that, we looked at the engraving of a person who was shot in the heart. We then started to walk back and found out St George's House used to be a pub called The Three Best Boys. Then, as we were walking up the pathway, there was a sign that said something about the park being built in 2015.

Finally, we came back to school and played for a bit.

## Gracie Critcher (8)

St George's CE Primary School, Wrotham

# Village Walk

Dear Diary,

Yesterday afternoon we were filled with anticipation because we were excited about going on a village walk. It took ages in our classroom while we were put in our groups but finally, we set off on our walk.

We went to the park and we were looking at the name. After that, we went to the oak tree which was planted in memory of Stephen Hollinshead. After that, we strolled to the churchyard. We looked at the grave with a rose on it.

After a while, we went to Ella's house to look at the vine plant. Then we walked up to St Mark's Road and found out that one of the cottages was a butcher's shop.

A little while later, we reached the Bull Hotel and looked at the different food plants.

Before long we started to make our way back to school. I was feeling very tired.

## Matthew Hodges (9)
St George's CE Primary School, Wrotham

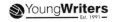
YoungWriters
Est. 1991

# The Village Walk

Dear Diary,

Yesterday I went on a walk through beautiful Wrotham with Year 3 and 4. By the way, I'm in Year 4. We went to Ella's house and I saw the Pinot Noir vine but sadly it wasn't in bloom. Eventually, I came across a famous oak tree that was planted for Noddy.

At the Bull Hotel, there were lots of plants. At the Bull Hotel, the plants were curry plants, lemon plants, apple mint plants and mint plants. Zac, Hassan, Dylan and I saw M&M's.

Someone called George Child was shot in 1988. My friends and I saw Roman numerals. Dylan saw his dad and went in his car. We also saw the Wrotham sign and I pretended to be an old man.

When I got back to school I thought about my favourite thing. My favourite thing was Ella's house.

**Teddy Dennis Henry Lingham (9)**
St George's CE Primary School, Wrotham

# My Wrotham Walk

Dear Diary,

First, we were reading which I find boring... Then suddenly, the parents came and I was full of anticipation because we were ready for the wonderful, natural, lovely walk around Wrotham. We headed off and I was not bored anymore and I saw some herbs at the Bull Hotel.

Then we went to the park and found out more facts. We walked with my mum, Nicholas, Lilly, Bella and Hillary and we found out what a Pinot Noir vine looks like. It's crusty, burnt and brown. I had achy legs and I had some of my mum's drink. I said, "Mum, are we going back to school yet?" We went to the graveyard and found a Roman stone. We then went back to school had breaktime.

## Holly Hayler (9)
St George's CE Primary School, Wrotham

# Wrotham Walk

Dear Diary,

Yesterday afternoon we were filled with anticipation because we were excited about going on a village walk. At the Bull Hotel, I silently looked for herbs. I looked for them quickly. I looked around and saw that it was curry night.

The old shop was a butcher's shop but was turned into a house. We next went to Pilgrims Way and went to a food court. Pilgrims Way is called this because in the olden days it was the road used to walk from London to Canterbury.

## Curtis Heather (8)

St George's CE Primary School, Wrotham

# The Incredible Diary Of... Hercules

Dear Diary,

King Eurystheus annoyed me so much I nearly walked off.

He said, "You have one more mission to do."

I set off on my last mission and thought, *hopefully, I will be free after this. That will make me happy.*

In the distance, I saw something shiny in the water and I dived to see what it was. It was a broken bank and something blue was inside it. It was a 100 electric eels. On the other side, there were 100 sharks and one of the sharks came over and stroked me. I stroked him back. The 100 sharks raced to the electric eels to try and kill all of them but it didn't work. There were only 25 sharks left and 45 electric eels. The sharks went down fast until there was just me and 45 electric eels. It was ages until the 45 eels went down.

The mission was to get the diamonds but they're hidden in rooms all over the broken bank. I only found one. I found that one in a disabled toilet in the sink. Then I found two and one was in a light. Another one was in my trouser pocket and one was in a little tank.

## Ronnie Richard Leslie (8)

West Minster Primary School, Sheerness

# The Incredible Diary Of... Hercules

Dear Diary,

Today King Eurystheus annoyed me so much! The horrible man told me I have to complete another task. Although I didn't want to do it, I set off to complete the task.

The journey was a very long walk. Eventually, I arrived at Floating Island behind the castle. Suddenly, the dragon appeared with the unicorn. The dragon started to try and hurt the unicorn. I felt really worried and scared because the dragon was really big and looked really scary with really sharp claws. I got my sword out and tried to cut it but it was a fail. I quickly went and hid and then thought of something.

Suddenly, when I was about to leave the castle I bumped into the king. I asked the king if he could help me kill the dragon and he said yes. Next, the king quickly went into a room and got a gun that shot out fireballs. We quickly ran out of the door and went up to the dragon and just looked at it. The king started shooting fireballs at it and with a big thud, the dragon fell to the floor. Suddenly there were two little dragons instead of one. I went up to the little ones and cut them with my sword and they fell to the floor.

Something shiny and shimmery caught my eye and I bent down and got it. I suddenly dropped it on a rock and the rock turned into ice. I quickly got a glove, picked it up and set off back to King Eurystheus. Feeling as excited as ever I reached the castle. I went into the castle and showed King Eurystheus the ice bone. Being as silly as ever, he jumped into his brass pot.

I quickly ran out of the castle and said to myself, "I'm free forever and ever now."

It was the best day ever!

## Tia Tooley (8)

West Minster Primary School, Sheerness

# The Incredible Diary Of...
# Hercules

Dear Diary,

Today King Eurystheus annoyed me more than ever before. I have to do another task. I have to kill a three-headed ogre that eats poisonous insects and big, hard rocks.

I started my journey and went through a cave and then went through some trees. I then had to go through a muddy puddle. King Eurystheus is the most annoying person in the land, but I finally got to where that rock ogre lives. He was sleeping in his cave. I tripped over a rock and made lots of noise. It woke up the ogre. My friends had to help me so I called them and we all shot it with everything we had, but we didn't kill it. Maybe it's because it's a rock. A rock was on the floor. I picked it up and threw it at the ogre and it fell to pieces. Suddenly, it started building back up again and it turned into thousands of rock ogres.

I ran into my hiding place and made a plan. I had to think about it for a moment. I thought of one and it was for the god Sekhmet to come and help me. She helped me poke her a stick through the ogre and chase her because she's a powerful god.

The ogres fell into pieces and my friends and I put them back in the cave before they could start building up again. We built rocks all over the cave so they couldn't get out.

In the distance, I saw something glowing. I ran over to it and it was a rock. I picked it up and pointed it at something and it turned into rock. I took it back to King Eurystheus. I showed him what it did and it made him jump so he went into his glass pot.

I finally got to get away from that horrible man that kept making me do task after task.

**Lexie Johnson (8)**
West Minster Primary School, Sheerness

# The Incredible Diary Of... Hercules

Dear Diary,

Yesterday, King Eurystheus made me so fierce that I nearly exploded. The wicked male made me do another task that was dangerous. I did not want to go but I went to complete the task.

It was long and hard but suddenly I reached the huge shipwreck in the ocean. The ship was old and really rusty. I felt a strange feeling I had never felt before. I climbed inside and saw an alarming creature. It was merciless to kill the despicable monster. The thing was colossal, mighty and terrifying.

I went to hide for a while in an old, empty rock cave. It was cold and breezy but I was safe.

After I came out of the cave I climbed back into the shipwreck and saw the rock-solid beast. I threw an arrow at the beast but it bounced right back. I was shocked. I didn't believe my eyes. I rubbed my eyes and the beast looked at me. The fish distracted the rest of the sharks but some of the fish sadly got eaten. The other sharks are huge but dumb. The fish helped me get the rock shell off of the shark when the other sharks biting him. When the shell fell off, I thanked the fish that survived.

I loaded the bow and arrow and shot over the sharks. A shark fell to the golden sand. I took the beetle-sized teeth for the task King Eurystheus gave me.

It took a very long time to get back to the palace. I reached the palace, went inside and showed the scales and teeth. He was scared and jumped in his brass pot. When he was in the pot, I ran away free forever.

## Amelia Rose Munday (8)
West Minster Primary School, Sheerness

# The Incredible Diary Of...
# Hercules

Dear Diary,
Today King Eurystheus made me so annoyed. He said that I had to do another task. I needed to save a baby snow wolf. I think it will be so cute. I set off and I came to a cold and chilly snow mountain. It was the coldest place ever. Feeling cheerful, I found some snow wolves, they were so cute. There were two of them. They looked like cute lions. It made me so happy that I started crying. I played with them a lot. I was so proud but suddenly one of the snow wolves pointed to another snow wolf that was trapped. I had to rescue it. The snow wolves were crying so loudly. It was so sad. I tried tying string but it was too weak and it broke straight away. I was so sad for the little snow wolf, it deserved more. Feeling upset, I remembered that I had a rope in my bag. I tied the rope around a big block of ice and the wolves threw it to the other snow wolf that was stuck. We did it with teamwork. I pulled the rope by myself but it didn't work. I asked another wolf and he helped me and it moved a bit but not a lot. We both asked the other wolf to help and all of a sudden it moved forwards, the snow wolf nearly fell off the ice.

They were so happy. We played with each other. It was so much fun. We were best friends forever. Eventually, I got out of that horrible castle and never saw King Eurystheus again. It was the best day ever.

## Tiana Johnson (8)
West Minster Primary School, Sheerness

# The Incredible Diary Of... Hercules

Dear Diary,

Today started badly because I was meant to be gone by now but King Eurystheus irritated me. He bellowed, "You need to slay a skyscraper-sized scorpion and the laser beam dolphins shooting lasers out of their eyes."

"Wow, that is terrifying, why me?" I barked to myself.

I went on my travelling adventure. I leapt in the pond as if I was a frog. I got to a sewer system and it was dreadful. There were rats and snakes. Luckily I have a lion's skin and it bothered them. Some snakes broke their teeth. I bet that hurt them so badly. Soon I got to the ocean. Next, I was tangled up in a pesky sea anemone. It tangled me up but I escaped.

I kept on diving down. Eventually, the scorpion glared at me. I tried slaying the beast but it didn't work. I saw a sunken ship and went in there to think of a plan.

"I know what to do, get the marine army. They have some information about the beast."

"Yes we do, you need to tie seaweed over the scorpion's eyes, then cut the beast's legs off. I cut the dolphins fins off with a lightsaber and for the beast, I used a knife.
I made the journey back and the king hopped in his vase.

## Arthur Michael Bancroft (8)
West Minster Primary School, Sheerness

# The Incredible Diary Of... Hercules

Dear Diary,

Today I was mad with King Eurystheus because he lied. There is a 13th labour to complete, it's a dreadful challenge.

Off I went to search but King Eurystheus stopped me to tell me the challenge was a megalodon that had red eyes and scars all over his body. I was scared about this megalodon. He must have had lots of battles with fish *and* people.

I thought for a bit. *Where could he be? In the Underworld,* I think because there were underwater craters.

I got there, put my snorkels on and dived down into the deep blue ocean. There were lots of lovely fish in the ocean. There was also an octopus that had a massive bite mark on him.

All of a sudden, the megalodon ate the little octopus. I felt sad for the octopus and rushed down to get closer and hit the megalodon with my trusty sword. He was larger than I expected. He had lots of bite marks on his body.

I swung my sword at his bite mark to hurt more but all that did was hurt it. I hit him again and this time I killed him.

## Alfie Preston (8)
West Minster Primary School, Sheerness

# Baby Goes On An Adventure

Dear Diary,

I was woken up by my mummy and this is the part I'm most excited for, breakfast! I'm two, I should at least be allowed chocolate or something good like that. Here we go, Mummy usually just gives the nasty green goo to me, huh? Instead, I got yummy yoghurt. *Mmm, yum. I can't wait to enjoy this.* Oh jackpot! I got a chocolate bar too. OMG I was so excited. What! Why did she take it? It was hers all along. *Waa-waa.* I had green gooey stuff in my mouth.

"Open wide."

Yep, I wasn't having that. *How about I turn my head around like this? How about that?*

We went to the park and my friends were there but it was really boring so I cried and guess where my mummy took me? To the toy shop. I saw a lovely bear toy so I wanted it. I said I wanted it, well... I didn't ask I just whined and I got it.

After that, I went home with my mummy and it was about 9ish so she put me to bed and I wasn't excited about tomorrow because it will happen again.

## Maicie Hill (10)
West Minster Primary School, Sheerness

# The Incredible Diary Of... The Long Ride

Dear Diary,

Today was one of the worst days of my life. Here's what happened...

It was an ordinary Saturday, at least that was what I thought. My annoying brother, Flash, kept pulling pranks on me so I decided to get my revenge by putting thousands of spiders on his bed. That turned out to be a big mistake because my mum was doing the bedsheets that day.

When my mum found out I did it I was grounded. We had to get out of the house. Honestly, I was fine with that. Then all of a sudden, I got a text from my friend. It said: 'Steam fighters two hours out'. Oh no, this was the day I was waiting for and I missed it. It was all my fault. I sat there like a little monkey crying.

After a while, I sat with a frown. Then my little brother, Dan, started crying so we had to pull over. Finally, we started the car. As quick as a flash my dad had a fight and from somewhere a police car pulled us over. We had an hour's talk and at last we went home but we had lost the keys.

## Anooshkan Anura Julian (10)

West Minster Primary School, Sheerness

# Please Mrs Butler

*(Inspired by 'Please Mrs Butler' by Allan Ahlberg)*

Dear Diary,
On Monday I said to my teacher,
"Please Mrs Butler,
This boy, Derek Drew
Keeps copying my work, Miss,
What shall I do?"

"Go and sit in a farm of pigs, dear,
Go and paint yourself pink,
Take your book in the cupboard of boom, my lamb,
Do whatever you think."

On Tuesday I said to my teacher,
"Please Mrs Butler,
This boy, Derek Drew
Keeps taking my rubber, Miss,
What shall I do?"

"Keep it in your ear, dear,
Hide it in your dress,
Flip it into your mouth, love,
Do what you think best."

On Wednesday I said to my teacher,
"Please Mrs Butler
This boy, Derek Drew
Keeps calling me rude names, Miss
What shall I do?"

"Stick yourself in the mud, dear,
Run away to a cup of tea,
Do whatever you can, my flower,
But don't ask me!"

**Joshua Smith (10)**
West Minster Primary School, Sheerness

# Please Mrs Butler

*(Inspired by 'Please Mrs Butler' by Allan Ahlberg)*

Dear Diary,
On Monday I said to my teacher,
"Please Mrs Butler,
This boy, Derek Drew
Keeps copying my work, Miss
What shall I do?"

"Go and sit on a tree, dear,
Go and sit on a drink,
Take your books on the seagull,
Do whatever you think."

On Tuesday I said to my teacher,
"Please Mrs Butler
This boy, Derek Drew
Keeps taking my rubber, Miss,
What shall I do?"

"Keep it in your smelly sack, dear,
Hide it on a guest,
Give it to a flying fish, love,
Do what you think best."

On Wednesday I said to my teacher,
"Please Mrs Butler
This boy Derek Drew
Keeps calling me rude names, Miss
What shall I do?"

"Put yourself in a sewage tunnel, dear,
Run away to a sea of tea,
Do what you can, my flower,
But don't ask me!"

**Evie Joan Reid (11)**
West Minster Primary School, Sheerness

# Please Mrs Butler

*(Inspired by 'Please Mrs Butler' by Allan Ahlberg)*

Dear Diary,
On Monday I said to my teacher,
"Please Mrs Butler
This boy, Derek Drew
Keeps copying my work, Miss
What shall I do?"

"Go and sit in the thinking spot, dear,
Go and sit in a drink,
Take your books to the sun, my lamb,
Do whatever you think."

On Tuesday I said to my teacher,
"Please Mrs Butler
This boy, Derek Drew
Keeps taking my rubber, Miss
What shall I do?"

"Keep it in your tray, dear,
Hide it in your chest,
Put it in your belly, love,
Do what you think best."

On Wednesday I said to my teacher,
"Please Mrs Butler
This boy, Derek Drew
Keeps calling me rude names,
What shall I do?"

"Put yourself in the rocket, my bee,
Run away to sea,
Do whatever you can, my flower,
But don't ask me!"

**Tyler Amos (8)**
West Minster Primary School, Sheerness

# The Incredible Diary Of...
# Hercules

Dear Diary,

Today was unbelievable. King Eurystheus gave me another task to do. I was so angry at King Eurystheus I did not know what to say, but I went on my horrible task anyway so I would be free from King Eurystheus.

I thought about it a bit to see where the witch was but it might be a lion, a bear, a snake or a gorilla or something that is silly and horrible.

I walked step after step but whatever the enemy was it would be invincible, terrible and strong. It would be the most horrible thing I had ever seen. I walked on and on but there was a lion that had sharp claws. I chopped its legs off and defeated it. I just kept on walking. I hoped I would never see anything like that again. If I did I would destroy it but then I had found the monster but was scared I wouldn't get it right. I tried to kill the witch with my sword. There were then three witches. I defeated the right witch and my task was completed.

## Hayden Zwolinski (8)

West Minster Primary School, Sheerness

138

# Fun Arcade

Dear Diary,

I jumped out of my bed with a grin on my face. I got dressed and ran out of my house. As I approached the ultra fun arcade, I saw the flashing lights shining on me. I could hear the sound of machines. All around me were bright games consoles. I had to adjust my eyes. My mouth started to water as I smelt the smell of fried onions travelling through my nostrils. *Beep, beep* went all the buttons. I could hear the little kids screaming at machines.

After playing several games I started to drift off. Suddenly, I saw my favourite game: Double Dragons. I ran over and started to play. The joystick was so loose it was a bit hard to play. I got my name on the leaderboard because I'm good at the game.

It was so fun today at this ultra fun arcade but it was time to go. I had only spent £10 at the arcade. I was sad I had to leave but it was near bedtime. I walked home.

## Taylor Sheppard (10)

West Minster Primary School, Sheerness

# Please Mrs Butler

*(Inspired by 'Please Mrs Butler' by Allan Ahlberg)*

Dear Diary,
On Monday I said to my teacher,
"Please Mrs Butler,
This boy, Derek Drew
Keeps copying my work, Miss
What shall I do?"

"Go and see in the bathroom, dear,
Go and sit in a drink,
Take your books to the sun, my lamb,
Do whatever you think."

On Tuesday I said to my teacher,
"Please Mrs Butler,
This boy, Derek Drew
Keeps taking my rubber,
What shall I do?"

"Keep it in your coat, dear,
Hide it up a dress,
Eat it, my love,
Do whatever you think best."

On Wednesday I said to my teacher,
"Please Mrs Butler
This boy, Derek Drew
Keeps calling me rude names, Miss
What shall I do?"

"Take yourself to the moon, dear,
Run away to a stream my dear,
Do whatever you can, my flower, but
Don't ask me!"

## Jersi Noel (9)
West Minster Primary School, Sheerness

# A Trip To The Arcade

Dear Diary,

*Beep! Beep! Beep!* The rattling sound of my alarm clock. All was dark, the beam off my lamp blinding me and slowly helping me regain my vision. I turned on the TV. Ah, it was so refreshing relaxing in bed and watching the... ads! Just the word I dread, 30 seconds, non-skippable ads. Actually, I was kind of bored this morning. I would love to do something fun. That was my plan for the day.

Just arriving, the rotten stench of vinegar went whooshing past. I knew this day could go either way. I walked toward the arcade. My jaw dropped. It was a forest of games. I was so excited my belly bubbled. I thought I had a sugar rush. What was that in the corner of my eye? It couldn't have been, but it was, the original Pac-Man.

I started to play. Ahh, the memories. Just going around as a yellow monster was amazing. I stayed there for hours. Hopefully, I will go back.

## Luke Stevens (10)

West Minster Primary School, Sheerness

# The Incredible Diary Of...

Dear Diary,

Today I returned to the tomb with my friend, Lord Carnarvon. I felt amazing because I had been looking for it for so long and I finally found it. I wondered if it was a trick but it wasn't, it was Tutankhamun.

We found the tomb when a little water boy was playing with sand and he found a rock step. He called me and I called the rest. We dug and dug and found twelve more steps. We then saw a door. I opened the door and saw a golden table, a book and more. Most of it was gold. In the corner, there were two statues of him. They were looking at a black door. We knocked it down. I heard nothing at all. It was Tut. I felt like I was going to explode.

I took a step forward and found Tut's coffin. It was amazing. I couldn't believe my eyes. I can't explain how amazing it was. I'm going to be famous. Can you believe it?

## Lilli-Rai Guyver (8)

West Minster Primary School, Sheerness

# The Incredible Diary Of... Middle School

Sunday

Dear Diary,

Today I was working on a project for the school fair... Let me tell you something. It was so annoying! I swear I would've raged if my mum shouted, "Dinner!" I knocked it over, let's just say I was really mad.

Monday

Dear Diary,

Today was the day where I had to show my project... I had an idea... *Do I have to show it?*

"Wake up, school time!" Mum said.

"I don't feel so well," I said.

"Don't try it, get up!" she shouted.

I woke up.

In school

Dear Diary,

"Hmmm, Ralph?" my teacher said.

I had to show my project but then a miracle happened... Basically, I threw up.

After that, I got sent home and my mum felt really bad... Looks like I'm not going to school again today.

## Tia Michelle Kelly Maria Morgan (10)
West Minster Primary School, Sheerness

# The Mystery Arcade

Dear Diary,

Today was one of the best days ever, I went to the new arcade in town with my auntie and no one has been in there yet. I'm going to be one of the first people to go in there, that's probably why it's called The Mystery Arcade.

Once we arrived, I was so excited because some games there are classics and I want to know how they were set and are they different from games of today?

Once we got our tickets we went inside and saw lots of arcade machines and I didn't know where to start.

As I was standing, trying to find a machine to go on, I found a machine, it was a game called NBA 2K19, a basketball game. I played it and it took me one hour and 30 minutes. I stopped playing it and my auntie and I went on 30 more games.

Then we left the arcade and went to Spoons for dinner. I could smell nachos covered in salsa.

## Shianne Berrisford (10)

West Minster Primary School, Sheerness

# The Incredible Diary Of... Hercules

Dear Diary,

I had the most bad-tempered day today. King Eurystheus made me angrier than ever before because he lied to me and said I still had another task to do. After this task though, I would never have to do another one again. I had to kill a killer whale.

Every time I bring something back to the castle, King Eurystheus jumps into a brass pot because it scares him every time. It takes me a long time to finish each task. I am fed up but I don't want to tell King Eurystheus, because then I won't be forgiven for murdering my children and I want to be forgiven otherwise I will be a bad-tempered person and everybody will call me a bad-tempered killer. My task is so, so, so super difficult and I had to use all my skills to complete my task.

I wish I had never killed my children now because I wouldn't be in all this mess.

## Poppy-May Duchense (7)
West Minster Primary School, Sheerness

147

# The MK Arcade

Dear Diary,

Today was one of the best days ever. I sprung out of bed and got dressed and flew out the door. I jumped into my auntie's car and we got going. When we arrived at the MK Arcade I was gobsmacked. I could see huge smiles on everyone's faces. There was a scent of fish and chips in the air. I could hear machines playing happy music and coins being won.

The best game I played when I was at the MK Arcade had to be Bloxel City because it was what I thought it would be, absolutely amazing. Auntie Tiff had a different opinion though, she was over at the karaoke machine with her BFF, Lisa, singing to Years & Years (If You're Over Me). I just acted like I didn't know her.

Once we got back home, I remembered two things... One, never let Tiff sing and two, go to MK Arcade!

## Maddie Kulinski (9)

West Minster Primary School, Sheerness

# How Hot Dogs Are Made

Dear Diary,

Today I'm going on a school trip to see how a hot dog is made in a factory. I was very excited and hungry on the way. I've just arrived at the factory and the first part of the process is that you grate the meat and put pressure on the meat to squash the bad stuff out. You then roll it up and put it in a boiler so it will keep its shape. The staff told us the next bit is when you pack the sausages in a jar with liquid to keep them juicy.

We next went to the bakery and there they made the buns. The first ingredient was flour, they then added water and mixed it up. Then they left it to cook.

Once it was cooked it was put in the fridge. Then the last bit is the packaging. A machine had plastic to cover the buns. That was the school trip over.

## Tristan Pay (9)

West Minster Primary School, Sheerness

# My Best Day At The Arcade

Dear Diary,

Well, that was one of the best days of my life. When I got there my jaw dropped into little pieces when I saw the 169 games in the Laser Zap Arcade. I ran to NBA2K19. When I got inside I saw games. It was dark like it was midnight. I saw flashing lights everywhere and there were Minecraft and lots of people there too.

I heard people shouting and saying, "I won!" I could smell vinegar and chips from the burger van across the road. Laser Zap Arcade was so much fun but then my friends went running off.

After I played NBA 25 times in a row I played sometimes else. I played 2p machines and I won a few sweets and tickets too.

I went home happy. I wanted to stay longer but if I did, I would play more games but I had the time of my life.

## Teddie William Pagett (9)

West Minster Primary School, Sheerness

# The Incredible Diary Of...

Dear Diary,

Maddie, my best friend, and I went to Maisey's Amazing Arcade. It was epic.

My mouth was watering because I could smell the hot, greasy nachos covered in salsa and cheese.

We went to get our tickets and I saw caramel apples. My eyes went bold.

I could hear all of the games and money coming out of the machines.

After a while, we played like a billion games but we didn't keep track. As we were searching for my favourite game I was disappointed because they didn't have it, but at least they had fun games. Some games I didn't even know about. It was the best experience ever! I wish I could go every day. We went home and I said, "Do you want to go back?"

I'm exhausted now, see you tomorrow.

## Maisey Jo Cooke (10)
West Minster Primary School, Sheerness

# The Heads Up Arcade

Dear Diary,

Today when I woke up my alarm clock went off. I had one of the best days ever. I went to an arcade called Heads Up Arcade. It was dark and had lots of bright, fun, exciting games. They might be a bit old but they were really fun and exciting.

One of my favourite things was the restaurant. They had pizza, chips, nuggets, burgers, milkshakes, fizzy juice and lots of other stuff, probably anything you want.

My favourite game was Double Dragon. I could hear buttons beep, the coins running down the machines and the children screaming happily. I could hear the noise of the tickets running down the machines. It was so cheap so I played lots more games. It was 50p a game. I was so shocked. I thought it would be £30 or more.

## Caitlin Harris (10)

West Minster Primary School, Sheerness

# Adventure To The Arcade

Dear Diary,

I opened my eyes whilst lying in bed wondering what to do. Then I thought I would go to Boom Arcade. I jumped out of bed with a big smile on my face. I had my breakfast and got ready and ran downstairs and out of the door as fast as I could. I got in the car with Mum and we drove to the arcade.

We finally arrived at Boom Arcade. We walked inside and my jaw dropped. I smelt the hot chips and hot doughnuts covered in sugar. It made my mouth water. I heard all the coins from the 2p machines. I played so many games. I played a lot of classics. My eyes started to droop. I played some new games as well. We left because I was so tired.

We left the arcade and arrived home. I was so tired but that was the best experience ever!

## Sophie Warwick (10)

West Minster Primary School, Sheerness

# A Life Of A Car

Dear Diary,

It is another boring day. Uh oh, please don't say children are coming in the car. It sounds like we are going for a long drive so I'm happy.

I went to Tesco first and while there I was getting thirsty so I beeped to tell my family to hurry up. They came running over so I told them I needed a drink so they asked if I wanted diesel or petrol and of course I chose diesel. It was so yummy.

After that, I found out we were going to a drive-through zoo. I was so shocked. I had been to a zoo before but I had to wait outside for four hours. I hope the monkeys don't do any funny business on me otherwise I won't be very happy! I'm most excited about the tigers. This was the best day of my life.

## Rosie McNeill (9)

West Minster Primary School, Sheerness

# The Incredible Diary Of... A Mermaid

Dear Diary,

Yesterday, King Eurystheus stressed me out so much that I couldn't even speak! That horrible, horrid, disgusting man told me that I had another long hard task. I was so tired I couldn't even walk. I didn't want to go because my legs were already aching but I had to set off so I did.

I travelled a long time just to see the awful, vicious jellyfish monster. Before I went out to see what I could do, I hid behind a statue to think.

A little while later, I thought, *what could I do?* I went out and I was scared but I killed it. Now I can peacefully have a nice day. I got away from King Eurystheus.

## Neelie Mcgow (8)

West Minster Primary School, Sheerness

# Please Mrs Butler

*(Inspired by 'Please Mrs Butler' by Allan Ahlberg)*

Dear Diary,
On Monday I said to my teacher,
"Please Mrs Butler,
This boy, Derek Drew
Keeps copying my work, Miss,
What shall I do?"

"Go and sit on the chair, dear,
Go and sit on the pink chair,
Take your book to the box, my lamb,
Do whatever you think."

On Tuesday I said to my teacher,
"Please Mrs Butler
This boy, Derek Drew
Keeps taking my rubber, Miss,
What shall I do?"

"Keep it in your bedroom,
Hide it in the chest,
Put it in the pot, love,
Do what you think best."

## Kaydon Mitchell (7)
West Minster Primary School, Sheerness

156

# The Incredible Diary Of... Hercules

Dear Diary,

Yesterday King Eurystheus said I had a task to do. I had to kill a snow dragon for its tooth for King Eurystheus.

I set off for the castle and arrived. I was nervous to go into the castle. I went into the castle to kill the dragon. I split the dragon in half, it split into two dragons. I hid in a big igloo and had a think. I prayed to the gods for help. The sun god shot a beam of light on the dragon and it was gone. I saw one of the little dragon's teeth in the distance, I picked it up. I put it in my bag and I walked back to the king and gave the tooth to him. He said I was finished.

## Dexter Wallis (8)

West Minster Primary School, Sheerness

# The Incredible Diary Of...

Dear Diary,

Today I returned to the tomb with my friend, Lord Carnarvon. I felt excellent because I was the first to go inside and I'm going to be famous. The stuff is going to be put in a museum and people will see it.

After we found the tomb I opened the door and I saw gold, statues, jewellery, a box, a golden chair and another chair. I felt excited because I've been looking for ages. I heard nothing but my footsteps. I took a step forward and discovered a second spinning wall. I pushed it and found Tutankhamun's body. I am so glad I found it.

## Isaac (8)

West Minster Primary School, Sheerness

# The Best Arcade Ever

Dear Diary,
Today I visited the best arcade in the whole entire universe. It has the best games ever and they were tempting me to go on every one. It was like a dream come true.
When I was at the arcade I could smell candyfloss all around me like a fragrance and other kids shouting yes and no from other games.
Other people looked very, very, very excited on the games which are good. It is the best arcade.
Today was the best day ever. The best arcade is the best arcade forever and ever.

## Sophie Emans (9)
West Minster Primary School, Sheerness

# The Incredible Diary Of...

Dear Diary,

Before I entered the tomb I felt excited because I had been looking for this tomb and then I finally found it.

We found the tomb when the supply person went to get some water and he hit a stone but it was no ordinary stone, it was a sticky stone with sand on it.

I opened the door and saw another door. I opened that door and I saw lots of jewellery and diamonds. I also saw another passageway. I felt curious about this passageway. I heard nothing at all except my heart beating.

## Malachi Sands-Roache (7)

West Minster Primary School, Sheerness

# Please Mrs Butler

*(Inspired by 'Please Mrs Butler' by Allan Ahlberg)*

Dear Diary,
On Monday I said to my teacher,
"Please Mrs Butler,
This boy, Derek Drew
Keeps copying my work,
What shall I do?

"Go and sit in the dandelions, dear,
Go and sit in the ink,
Take your book to the library, my lamb,
Do whatever you think."

On Tuesday I said to my teacher,
"Please Mrs Butler
This boy, Derek Drew
Keeps taking my rubber, Miss,
What shall I do?"

## Millie Starling (8)
West Minster Primary School, Sheerness

# The Incredible Diary Of... Hercules

Dear Diary,

Yesterday I was told by King Eurystheus that I must do another task. I was furious because I had to kill a snow dragon!

I set off to the Ice Land. When I arrived I saw a big castle. I walked into it and it was dark. A big snow dragon furiously roared and I chopped it in half and killed it.

## Joe Anthony Welch (8)

West Minster Primary School, Sheerness

162

# Young Writers Information

We hope you have enjoyed reading this book – and that you will continue to in the coming years.

If you're a young writer who enjoys reading and creative writing, or the parent of an enthusiastic poet or story writer, do visit our website **www.youngwriters.co.uk**. Here you will find free competitions, workshops and games, as well as recommended reads, a poetry glossary and our blog. There's lots to keep budding writers motivated to write!

If you would like to order further copies of this book, or any of our other titles, then please give us a call or order via your online account.

Young Writers
Remus House
Coltsfoot Drive
Peterborough
PE2 9BF
(01733) 890066
info@youngwriters.co.uk

Join in the conversation!
Tips, news, giveaways and much more!

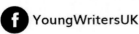 YoungWritersUK     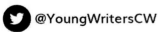 @YoungWritersCW